A Demc.. .
My Kitty

Werewolves, Vampires, and Demons, Oh My

Eve Langlais

New York Times and USA Today Bestselling author

EVELANGLAIS.COM

Copyright

Chapter One

The misogynistic ass at TDCM—short for the Thaumaturgic Department for the Concealment of Magic—looked down his haughty nose at me. It made me itch to give him a wart, right on the pointy tip.

Tucking my hands behind my back, I didn't give in to temptation. Not yet. I reserved the right to change my mind if he continued to piss me off.

"What do you mean I can't go in? I'm part of the investigative group studying the demonic incursion." The only woman amidst a bunch of snotty male wizards. They weren't impressed that I, a mere human witch, had been elected—by the High Coven—to work with them. To be fair, I really didn't want to work with the jerks either; however, that was beside the point. They were trying to block me.

Mr. I'm-So-Impressed-With-Myself sneered. "Your services are no longer needed, as the matter to which you refer is being handled by those properly suited to the task."

In other words, they'd found a way to oust the mangy human witch, and the university-educated wizards were taking charge of the investigation. Did I mention they were pompous, convinced of their superiority, and if something didn't fit their narrow definition then it didn't exist?

Humanity was so screwed.

I leaned forward and placed my hands on the reception desk rather than slapping him silly. "You can't be serious. I have valuable information to offer. Have you all forgotten I helped handle the library event and that I was there when the Peabody incident went down?" And by incident, I meant a house haunted by unknown forces that possessed the owner, got rid of the wife, and caused widespread problems since the possession turned out to be rather contagious.

"There were wizards on the scene as well. They will provide insight, if required, to the committee."

Insight? Snort. I highly doubted that, especially since no one had yet been able to answer any of the many questions arising from that incident, like why I, and the others, had lost a good fifteen minutes of time.

I remembered arriving at the Peabody house, and then I blinked and there was just a smoldering ruin where it used to stand.

No one knew what had happened. Not even Morfeus, the biggest asshat of the wizarding group currently blocking me.

I couldn't say I was entirely surprised. Morfeus and his cronies didn't want to explore what had occurred at the Peabody place. Something had happened, something they couldn't explain, and their pea-sized brains couldn't handle it. They were happy the house blew up. Most of them went *good riddance, problem solved.*

But I couldn't be content and just let things go. What if blowing it up wasn't enough? What if the demons—or whatever it was possessing non-magical folk—came back? I didn't want that. Especially since I'd seen what happened to witches hunted by demons.

Turned out we—as in witches, those born of human parents and bearing magic—were a tasty treat to them. A jelly-filled donut they liked to munch on. Some of the people who'd died were my friends, and since my life goals didn't include feeding a demon, I tended to have a vested interest in ensuring it didn't happen to me.

I also owed it to my coven to make sure it didn't happen to any more members. Losing witches meant fewer fees to help pay the rent on our coven headquarters.

And when I say coven, I should add that we don't dance around fires buck-naked praying to Satan. Nor do we have major orgies—a letdown for many applicants. At least once they were told, it tended to weed out the less serious.

So what did a coven of witches do? Other than moral support, we tended to get together for spell potlucks where we exchanged recipes, shredded ingredients, cooked up a bunch of potions in our cauldrons, and then went our merry ways until the next full moon or All Hallows' Eve.

Being a witch was less exciting than people thought.

We were also discriminated against.

"Listen here, bud." I leaned in closer, my fingers curling into fists on his desk. "I am the witch liaison for this sector, which means you can't shove me out of an active investigation involving us." Actually, the wizards probably could. Witches were barely recognized by the so-called true magic users. Our diluted bloodlines were an embarrassing reminder that their ancestors had once frolicked with humans.

Mr. Snooty didn't look impressed, nor did he change his mind. "Your coven will receive a report with the investigating group's findings once they've completed it."

"And how long will that take?" Uttered with the deepest sarcasm I could manage. Having dealt with the TDCM and its various sub-branches before, I knew it meant months, maybe more given their track record.

"Our best wizards are working on it."

"Working on it?" I couldn't help a high note of annoyance. "People are dying now."

"Actually, ever since the Peabody incident, there have been no new reported cases."

True, but I for one wasn't fooled. The demons had found a way into our world. They might be lying low for the moment, but I doubted it would last.

"You're a moron," I muttered as I spun on my heel, meaning to stomp out.

As departures went, it might have been more impressive if I hadn't bounced off a chest. A big and solid chest that sent me flying and landing, quite unceremoniously, on my ass.

The asshat at the desk snickered, which didn't help my temper.

A snarl might have curled my lip. "Watch where you're going."

"Terribly sorry," a cultivated male voice said, low and sexy. "I'm afraid I didn't notice you."

I looked up, way up, and got treated to chiseled perfection. Square chin. Bright, dancing, blue eyes. Blond hair. Wearing a casual outfit.

Obviously not a wizard. He'd have knocked me down and walked on past.

Still, how did he not notice me? Did my flame-red hair not register?

"Oh, don't worry about it. I just love polishing the floor with my butt." There might have been a liberal dose of sarcasm in there as I wiggled around.

He reached out a hand, again, his polite manners giving away the fact that he wasn't a magic-using douchenozzle. But if he wasn't a wizard, then what was he?

I felt a definite tingle when he grabbed my hand. A sizzle that made my girly parts sing va-va-va-voom. Since that never happened, I immediately assumed he wore a spell to make him more attractive to the opposite sex. So many men nowadays resorted to charms and magic instead of something old-fashioned like good manners.

Without any effort on his part, he hauled me to my feet, but once I was upright, he didn't release my hand.

I should have tugged it away; however, I found myself rather fascinated. "Are you an elf?"

Rude, yet I couldn't contain my curiosity.

At the query, his lips quirked. "Not exactly. And don't let my parents hear you even hint at it. They'd be most insulted."

Offended to be compared to what many believed was the most prestigious race in existence? Elves and wizards, and even shapeshifters and vampires were no longer a secret to the world. Humans had found out about them by accident via a televised incident that no amount of claims stating it was doctored could appease.

The supernaturals, as we humans tended to call them, those fascinating mystical creatures and beings we read about in fairy tales and legends, were real.

And obnoxious.

We lived in interesting times. With interesting people. And things that didn't quite classify as people but demanded rights.

The poor human governments were quite stymied. Especially when some of the more reclusive groups, such as the merfolk, began to demand tariffs on all goods floated on their seas. Apparently, the humans had been taking advantage of their oceans and abusing their waters for too long. The merfolk were quite done with humanity's disdain for their oceanic territory.

They hadn't quite declared war yet, but some of the more egregious infractions—a tanker ship leaking oil and doing nothing about it, plus the whaler that was overfishing the waters off the coast of Newfoundland—became the first convicted casualties of the newly enforced Poseidon Laws.

There was no appealing the decision. The Kraken ate the offending parties whole.

Being a somewhat morbid spirit at times, I kind of wondered if someone got to yell, "Release the Kraken!" Wrong, and yet I felt no sympathy. Humans had been abusing the world for too long. It was about time someone did something about it.

Of course, there were those that screamed it was our right to do as we pleased. Humans were the dominant race according to them. Humans made the rules.

The supernaturals, in many cases, refused to acknowledge them, and there was no true way of enforcing the laws short of declaring war. There were some that argued we should.

We lived in divided times.

As my mind wandered through the various species I knew of, trying to fit the hot and mysterious man into one of those groups, I realized he still held my hand. He also exhibited an amused glint in his eyes.

There goes Willow with her head in the clouds again. That was one of the nicer things kids had said about me when I was young. Those that chose to use meaner words? They got diarrhea in class. Bullying a witch, even a young one training in secret, was never a good idea.

I tugged my hand free—the loss of contact quite sobering—and I drew myself to my five feet five inches and a half, the half being important when you're short—and stated, in a haughty, if high-pitched voice, "I'd say thank you, but if you weren't so oblivious, this could have been avoided."

"My apologies again. My mind was preoccupied with other matters."

Probably on where to have lunch. Someone this good-looking probably never entertained a serious thought.

Ooh, that is mean, even for me. I shouldn't let my bad mood over getting kicked out of the demon investigation turn me into a bitch. "If you'll excuse me, I was just leaving."

"Going so soon? We just met." His lips quirked into a smile that made my girly bits tingle.

I armored myself against it and clutched the medallion at my neck, which wasn't doing its usual job of filtering out magic. Maybe the spell on it needed refreshing.

"I have business elsewhere." Namely my crummy coven office in the warehouse district. I rented a rundown building for my group with concrete floors perfect for drawing protective circles—and also not easily ignited. When spells went wrong, fire usually followed.

"Until we meet again, fair lady." He inclined his head and moved past me to the reception desk. I almost turned to watch. A red-blooded woman, I wanted to see if the rear presented itself as nicely as the front.

However, I restrained myself. Barely. If only I had the same self-control when it came to chocolate.

Chapter Two

While Alistair would have liked to detain the witch—somewhere more private where he could truly speak to her—to do so would have invited suspicion. Especially since he'd intentionally stood in her path in order to meet her.

What he'd not expected was for her to fall. It didn't exactly set the proper tone. But there was nothing he could do about that now. At least he'd managed to get a first impression.

Very attractive. Most definitely human. Humming faintly of magic. And did he mention attractive?

With her generous curves, fiery red hair, and snapping green eyes, she definitely stood out.

She also had attitude.

While Alistair would have liked to pursue the intriguing witch to continue their discourse, he had business here.

Business that could not wait.

The reception desk for the TDCM—which the humans mistakenly assumed was for The Defense and Care of Mammals—was manned by a portly fellow with a face that would have looked better with Alistair's fist in it.

Alistair's mood might have been somewhat

shaped by the conversation he'd overheard. Insane that in this day and age such discrimination still happened. Human witches might not have the same magical strength as those with pure elven or other blood, but they deserved the same respect as any other magic user. After all, it meant, somewhere down the line, one of the species had frolicked with a human.

But most wished to pretend that embarrassment hadn't happened—even if it continued to occur, just with fewer accidents.

It always baffled Alistair how the races treated the witches. Their skills were invaluable in many ways, not to mention pissing off the humans seemed rather shortsighted given they outnumbered non-humans about one hundred to one.

The fellow at the desk shot him a bored stare. "State your name and business."

"Alistair Fitzroy."

"Never heard of you." The man didn't even look down to check his tablet.

No wonder the redheaded lass was in such a temper. Such intolerable rudeness.

Alistair leaned closer. "I didn't ask if you'd heard of me. You will let me in. I am expected."

The other man eyed him up and down. "Maintenance crew are supposed to use the back entrance."

Pompous fool. He really had no idea who he messed with. "I am not with maintenance, and your attitude shall be reported. I am Alistair Fitzroy, and I was sent by La Fratellanza Di

Magia,"—the brotherhood of magic based out of Italy—"because of my expertise in ancient languages."

"You're the expert?" The receptionist eyed him up and down. "We expected someone older."

"You must be thinking of my father. He has, however, retired, and I am now taking his place. If you're done causing me delay…" Alistair inclined his head toward the doors behind the desk, guarded by spelled runes to keep out the riffraff.

Alistair could have busted in, but that wouldn't endear him to the TDCM, or anyone else for that matter.

"If you'll sign here." By sign, the man meant place his thumb on a parchment he slid out of a drawer to register his essence.

With a sigh of annoyance, Alistair imprinted his thumb on the paper and then snapped, "Could you move a little faster? In my country, we don't make our honored guests wait."

The rebuke served its purpose. "Just following the rules, Mr. Fitzroy—"

"That's Grande Mago Fitzroy to you." At times like these, when dealing with pompous idiots, tossing out a title could prove useful.

With the man put properly in his place, Alistair got a deferential head bob and a scurrying apology as the man stood from his desk and ushered Alistair past. "If you would come this way. Through this door, you'll find the lift to the third floor and the investigative offices. Grand Whizziar Morfeus is the one heading this particular case."

"I know." Alistair knew everything there was to know about the demonic problem plaguing this city. It was one of many in the world suddenly dealing with the body-snatching demons. The planets had aligned. Hell was coming to Earth.

But that wasn't common knowledge, yet.

The TDCM offices were like any other modern building, he noted as he finally got past the moron at the desk. Lots of gray industrial carpet, grayer walls, chrome finishes, and, hidden in the hanging artwork, runes.

While humans rarely got to set foot in the inner sanctum, the magical community had hidden for so long that they'd implemented necessary spells into their design. Spells such as *look away, you don't see a man with pointy ears or a green-skinned goblin.*

Oddly enough, though most of the hidden races had chosen to emerge into the public eye, some had elected to stay hidden. Vampires for one. They claimed that too many movies made them out to be the bad guys, and while *Twilight* had done much to elevate their status, they still preferred to stay in the shadows. Then there were the wizards, who liked secrecy and games. They also chose to remain a secret, more because they thought themselves too important to care what humans thought.

Soon, no one would be able to hide. It was only a matter of time before technology and an unexpected video outed them.

Taking the stairs because Alistair didn't believe in the modern practice of enclosed boxes that rose on a pulley system, he made it to the third floor quite easily.

It didn't prove hard to find the office he needed—it was the one with a voice bellowing from it.

"No. We are not contacting that hearth witch for information. We were all present. We know what we saw."

A voice murmured, and whatever they said caused another loud outburst. "I said no, and that is final."

Final according to him, not according to Alistair. It didn't take a genius to guess that the witch he'd met downstairs was the one being argued about. If she did have information, then he would gladly question her. Over dinner and a drink.

With a firm knock, he announced his presence.

The door was whipped open. A tall and gangly fellow poked his head out. "Who are you?"

"Is that the tea and biscuits?" asked someone else from within the room.

"No. Just some maintenance fellow who is lost. You have the wrong room." The reed-thin guy went to close the door, but Alistair had endured quite enough from fools already today.

He blocked the door and shoved it open, sending the guy stumbling.

"Just because I am not wearing robes or a suit doesn't make me maintenance," Alistair barked. "I am also not in the wrong place. I am here because my presence was requested."

"I requested tea and biscuits, not some male

model," announced the man who'd been yelling but a moment ago.

Alistair took in his appearance; as was the case with most elves, the rude fellow stood rather tall. He was gray-haired, the strands combed back and held in a queue at his neck. The sharp features and porcelain skin tone hinted at a strong elvish background, yet he wasn't pure. His round ears, hidden by hair, yet not peaking at the tips gave that away. He wore a suit, the pale yellow linen of his shirt matched by the striping in his gray tie.

Alistair's lip curled. "You must be Morfeus."

"I am Grand Whizziar Morfeus. Who are you? How dare you interrupt important matters."

Alistair tucked his hands behind his back. "As mentioned, my presence was requested. La Fratellanza Di Magia sent me. I am Fitzroy."

"You're too young to be Fitzroy." A frown creased Morfeus's brow.

"You're thinking of my father. He retired."

"I wasn't informed of this."

"Because you didn't need to know," Alistair remarked.

"And you're here to what, take his place?" Mockery hued the words, and Alistair could have taken offense, except...*I am better than he is.*

"I am as knowledgeable as, if not more learned than, my father when it comes to ancients languages and forgotten histories. Now, are we going to indulge in a boring exchange of credentials, or shall I do what I came here for? I was told you had something that no one could decipher."

Morfeus struggled, wanting to assert his superiority, yet at the same time, refusing to show Alistair what he'd come to do would make him appear weak and petty. "It's gibberish," he finally declared.

Gibberish that couldn't be photographed or drawn. There'd been many attempts. Even live videos failed to show it. Fascinating stuff. It meant Alistair had had to travel here in person to see it.

"Are you an expert in languages?" Alistair asked. "Have you studied ancient Babylonian and the lost language of the Hunnic? Are you versed in the dead scripts of the Eteocretan?"

"No, but—"

Alistair interrupted. "There is no *but*. You are not qualified to speak on this subject. Only I am. You would do well to stick to the things you can do. Like perhaps finding out where that tea and those biscuits have gone to." Petty perhaps, but enjoyable.

"You can't speak to me like that. I am a—"

"Step below me in status. I know. And yet, I am allowing you to speak freely. Or would you prefer we turn this gathering more formal and use our proper titles?" Alistair arched a brow, his lips pulled in a half smirk.

The other men in the room, three besides Morfeus, fought to restrain their snickers while Morfeus turned a shade of red that probably wasn't healthy.

"You can't speak to me like that. I am a Grand Whizziar."

"Which is below a Grande Mago, which means I can and will speak to you any way I like. The World Council of Mages has put me in charge of this investigation due to your lack of findings."

"They did not!" he exclaimed.

"Oh, I assure you, they have. Apparently, they could no longer ignore your incompetence."

"You lie. If that were true, they would have—" A flurry of ringtones went off, from a delicate bird chirping to the honk of a boat.

Alistair ignored them as the wizards present whipped out their phones to check the urgent message. He tucked his hands behind his back as he studied his new workspace. The office was boring with its pale gray walls, and small. It also lacked a decent view. Nothing like his usual quarters, but it would have to do.

He'd have Morfeus clean out his things—after the pompous fool fetched their refreshments.

"I don't believe it."

"Believe what?" Alistair asked with fake innocence.

"I'm to give you my office while you are heading the investigation and offer you any assistance you might require. There must be a mistake." Morfeus couldn't have looked more appalled.

Alistair, though, felt quite gleeful. "No mistake, and mighty kind of you to step down while those more qualified handle things." Alistair rubbed his hands together. "Now that we've settled that, I think we need more than tea and biscuits. Fetch us some sandwiches, would you? No crusts.

And on fresh bread. We've got a lot of work to do."

It wouldn't be long before the next demon attack occurred, and he wanted to be ready to meet it.

Chapter Three

Is TDCM right? Were the demon attacks really going to stop? My gut, and a healthy dose of paranoia, had me convinced we'd just seen the start of it.

For once, I wanted to be wrong. Demons weren't good for anyone. Not humans, wizards, and most especially witches.

So why then was the college of wizards, and the idiots running things, so determined to cut off their noses to spite their faces? How could they let their dislike of my impure origins prevent them from collaborating with me? We were on the same side. We both wanted to stop demon attacks.

Didn't we?

What possible reason could they have for not wanting to stop the possession of household pets and humans by parasitic entities?

What if they want to eliminate witches? Their disdain for us ran deep, but surely even they wouldn't stoop to allowing our savage murder?

Demons didn't just enjoy witch blood. Any magical blood would do. I'd seen one snack on the head doofus, Morfeus, at a library incident. The demons have only come after witches so far—easy prey—but what about when witches became scarce? Guess who they would turn to next?

Maybe if a few wizards got munched on, they'd change their tune. Not that I wished it on them. I didn't wish getting ripped apart and eaten by demons on anyone. Except for the jerk who'd broken into my car and stolen my *Guardians of the Galaxy* CD. I hoped he burned in a special place in Hell.

If the TDCM thought themselves too good for me, then screw them. I'd work on my own. I had resources. Perhaps not the same ability to grease palms as Morfeus and his crew, but I'd amassed a fair amount of friends over the years. As for those who couldn't be bought? They could be cursed. I never claimed to be a good witch.

I pulled my car—a tiny little eco-friendly thing—into the chain-linked yard that passed as a parking lot. It had no lines and was covered in gravel. Paving it proved an expense I just couldn't afford, and my landlord almost had a heart attack laughing when I asked.

Exiting my vehicle, I stretched and popped my limbs. My vehicle lacked the size and comfort of other cars, but I liked to think I did my small part to help the Earth.

It didn't hurt that my cousin Vinny had gotten it for me at a sweet, factory-price deal.

Pulling my satchel from the trunk—just about the only thing that would fit in it—I turned to survey my office. The official coven headquarters for this sector—which covered five states.

Sounded impressive, right?

Wrong. The reality wasn't anything close.

The warehouse looked depressing in daylight. Gray sheet metal exterior dotted with dirty windows, blacked out from the inside. A few of them were missing panes, teenagers having thrown rocks at them until they learned better—my windows tended to throw back, harder. That missing glass was covered in plywood.

Hard to believe this ugly excuse of a building was the headquarters for the Glas Cailleach, one of the biggest covens in the United States.

Biggest, and yet the youngest witch ran it. With me being just over thirty years of age, many had argued that I didn't have the maturity to manage a group this size. But none could deny I had the magic. The trials they'd put me through made that clear.

It also helped that no one wanted to deal with the pompous fools at the TDCM offices, except for me. Apparently, I was a sucker for punishment.

Entering, my male secretary—because today's world had an excess of men and a lack of women, some weird biological thing that scientists couldn't figure out—looked up from his computer. The glasses perched on the tip of his nose were a bright red today, the frames contrasting with Kal's ebony hair and green eyes.

A good-looking guy, Kal didn't lack for companionship. With the world population tipping in the Y chromosome area, the stigmas against homosexuals had finally been eradicated.

People were now free to love whomever they wanted, and if you were a woman and wanted more than one guy?

Well, hell, there were tax breaks if you did your part to keep the population happy and growing.

Not me, though. I wasn't ready to settle down with a reverse harem and pop out babies like so many of my friends had. Not that I was averse to the idea of children, more like I'd yet to find a man I wanted to have any with.

At the risk of sounding totally snobby, considering how much I hated Morfeus and his haughty gang of wizards, I wasn't sure I could settle for a regular ol' human.

I had magic at my fingertips. I could do incredible things. Impossible things. I kind of wanted my kids to inherit that ability, not to mention a guy I could share that with.

According to my mother, I needed to stop being so picky.

"Have I introduced you to Frederick yet?" Frederick was my mother's eighteen-year-old and single neighbor. Then there was Billy, the Geek Squad guy who came to fix her computer on a regular basis because she refused to put her coffee in a travel mug. And don't forget Stavros. Sure, he was pushing eighty with great-grandkids, but he'd just buried wife number three.

I don't need help finding a man. Men were bountiful. Men that weren't jerks or only after sex? Those were much rarer. Scarcer even than unicorns, which it turned out were quite plentiful once they stopped hiding.

Perhaps Mother had a point. Maybe I did need help. After all, when was the last time I went on a date?

The fact that I couldn't remember didn't bode well.

"So, we got a call from the TDCM," Kal announced.

"Did they change their mind about having me on their taskforce?" I asked. Maybe they realized the error of their ways.

Ha. Pigs would fly before that happened.

But didn't a lab claim to have grown wings on a pig?

The world needed a better expression.

"The call had nothing to do with the case. They wanted to know if you were going to have a plus one for the ball."

Only if Hell froze over. "Are you freaking kidding me?" As if I didn't have better things to worry about than some stupid ball.

As head of the coven, I was expected to attend. After all, my witchy ancestors had fought for their right to be recognized by the supernatural groups and not be burned at the stake.

If I were to be completely honest, the ball wasn't completely horrible. I got to hobnob with some really interesting people because it wasn't just wizards that attended but also folks from all supernatural walks of life.

All kinds. Since the event usually took place at the Atlantis—a newly built establishment for the supernatural with the world's largest aquarium—

even the merfolk deigned to attend. Although they did grumble about being forced to have their females wear bathing suit tops. Apparently, it went against their aquatic beliefs. But for the comfort of those who didn't believe in nudity, they complied and hid the nipples. Which led to a movement that protested, topless of course, with signs that said *Free the Boobies.*

"What should I tell them?" Kal asked. "Apparently, they need a final head count for the caterers."

Tell them my love life sucks. The only guy I could think of on short notice was sitting in front of me and would probably end up in a corner making out with a high-ranking elf.

For some reason, I thought of the blond hottie I'd met that morning. I'd bet he'd look pretty good in a tux. However, even I wasn't desperate enough to hunt him down and ask him to be my date.

Yet.

Things could change, though. With demons invading our world, who knew what the future held? I might decide I needed one last hurrah.

"How about I hold off on replying," was Kal's diplomatic suggestion.

I shook my head. "The ball is in less than a week, I doubt I'll have a date in that short of time. Tell them no." I'd fly solo, just a desperate witch in a dress forced to shave her legs and wedge her feet into heels.

Shit. Speaking of a dress… I still had to go shopping for one since it was considered quite gauche to wear the same one year after year. Obviously, a rule enacted by folks who could afford to buy expensive gowns they would wear only once.

I mentally added shopping to my growing list of things to do.

At this rate, I'd never find a man. Perhaps it was time to let my mother meddle in my love life.

Ack. Perish the thought.

"Did anything turn up on the Peabody autopsy?" The man who'd owned the house that blew up was the first human to show signs of possession. Previous reports had them inhabiting the bodies of cats and, in one case, a squirrel.

With the realization that they could possess humans, it elevated the urgency of the problem. Especially since we hadn't found a way to shove the demon out yet.

Exorcism? Made the entity laugh.

Magic? Made it giggle. *It tickles.*

The color red? Made those possessed go ballistic.

Peabody, our first case of possession in a human, had tried to eat a nurse with a red hair clip at the mental institution they'd sent him to for observation. A sound decision at the time, considering Peabody kept claiming his house was eating people. Turned out, it was true, but even if someone had immediately believed him, it wouldn't have saved Peabody. By then the demon had already attached itself to him.

Wizards, witches—aka me—and even priests had done their best to oust the spirit from his body. Everything failed, and in the end, Peabody had ended up succumbing to his demonic affliction.

When Peabody died—hung in his room with a bedsheet, which was quite the feat considering he had nothing tall to suspend from— the TDCM confiscated the body, fudging the paperwork for the humans to make it seem as if he'd been cremated.

In reality, the corpse ended up at a secret supernatural lab where it was dissected, first by magic and then by scalpel.

I'd been waiting on the results.

Kal shook his head. "Still nothing. They are holding the results tight."

"What about Sylvia?" My usual contact at Fairy Fingers—disguised as a physiotherapist's building, but what was, in actuality, a TDCM satellite office that handled lab work. Sylvia manned the reception desk for Fairy Fingers, and while a bit of an uptight snob, she had a weakness for my grandmother's fudge.

"Unfortunately, she's still on vacation for another week. Her replacement is not as cooperative."

Great. Just great. I'd hit a dead end, and it wasn't even lunch yet.

I spent the day going through the same reports. Poking my network of spies, which poked back and said they were on to something but not telling me what. I spent some time staring at the map I'd pinned on the wall. The tacks peppering it were multi-colored.

Red for confirmed dead witches by violent means.

Blue for possible demon activity—i.e., household pets going missing, desecration of churches and graveyards.

And green for missing supernaturals. Which happened a lot more lately since the humans found out about them. Considering the difficulty humanity had with multiculturism, the addition of people who weren't normal by their definition really proved difficult for them to accept. Although, in a positive bit of news, humans had stopped their war against each other because of religious beliefs and skin color. They now had a common enemy.

Sales of books titled *How to Defend Yourself Against Werewolves, One Hundred and One Ways To Make Your Garden Unattractive to Fairies,* and *Hiding Among You: How to Spot a Ghoul Neighbor* shot through the roof.

Sporting goods stores loved the tension in society. Most now offered an expanded selection of axes, machetes, crossbows, and, of course, silver ammunition.

That wasn't to say all humans wanted to identify and murder supernaturals, but a good chunk did.

Unfortunately for them, those that had emerged from the closet weren't about to quietly go away.

Given the rising tension, the upcoming Atlantis ball would be more important than ever for me to gauge the mood of the different factions.

Was the world about to go to war over their right to exist? Or would humans and supernaturals band together in a fight against demons?

It would make for an epic movie if they did.

And here I'd let myself get distracted from my current task. Where were the demons coming from?

I'd researched them at length, poring through ancient tomes, dusty with age, the pages brittle, the writing faded. A fair amount of time had been spent online, searching through articles, but the information varied widely. There wasn't one general consensus about demons. There were dozens, hundreds. Everyone had an opinion, but no one seemed to provide concrete fact.

Fact or fiction? It was thought you could only summon a demon through a serious of rituals.

Truth? I'd yet to speak to anyone who could confirm that worked. Possibly because stupidity got them killed.

Another fiction was that no one knew if the binding circles you saw in the movies worked to contain a demon. I liked to think they would because witches often used circles to protect themselves.

No matter who you were, wizard or witch, magic had to be wielded properly. The slightest misstep and bad things could happen. Marie-Anne never did grow back her hair.

While wizards could wield forces without outside help, witches had to rely on additional assistance, like a familiar—cats being the most popular—to focus. Wands or staffs were also quite common, and because our magic was more elusive, potions and ritual were of utmost importance.

The biggest question was, were we a match for demons?

The ones we'd encountered thus far were tough to beat, but so far, we'd prevailed. Against single demons. What would happen if we met several at once?

The Bibles showed Hell on Earth if the legion were to be unleashed.

They also depicted demons as towering, horned creatures. The demons we'd met up until now were hybrid creatures—half-demon, half-host body. Could they survive in our world without possessing someone or something?

Thus far, all the cases seemed to indicate the latter. The first cat case we'd become aware of—the one that ate its owner and her witchy friends, too—and then Peabody. The other cases I'd marked on the board also involved Earthly bodies taken over.

I only had a hunch so far, but it seemed to me the longer the demon hijacked a body, the more they could revert to their own form. Kind of like a werewolf, they could swap shapes at will.

Yet, not all of them could. Peabody never did manage to lose his human visage completely.

Could the reason be more nefarious than the length of their stay? Could the amount of magical blood they ingested—i.e., how many witches they ate—be the key to them being able to walk the Earth, terrorizing the innocent?

Morbid questions to be asking, but I wanted

to know.

Leaning back in my chair, I spun around and sighed.

Then squeaked as a very male voice said, "Am I interrupting?"

Opening my eyes, I took a moment to gape at tall and sexy standing in my office door. "What are you doing here?" Why had he come to my office? By he, I meant the blond guy I'd bumped into at the TDCM.

How did he even know where to find me? We hadn't exchanged names or anything else.

"I am hoping you'll accept my invitation to dinner."

Yes. Yes. My body said go for it, but my lips instead replied, "No." I didn't have time to go out for dinner with a super handsome guy.

I could almost hear my mother's shocked voice, *"Make time!"*

Of course, I revised my decision when the man said, "Are you sure? Because I was under the impression you wished to remain informed about the progress of the demonic incursion investigation."

My gaze narrowed. "What do you know about that?"

Then he floored me.

"I'm the man they put in charge of it."

Chapter Four

The lovely redhead—that he'd tracked down with ease given her name was in the files he'd taken over—blinked for a moment, her dark lashes framing her lovely clear, green eyes.

"Excuse me, but I thought Morfeus was in charge."

"He was." Alistair smiled. "But he's not anymore."

"But how? Why?" Her brow knit, but she still looked stunning. What a stroke of luck that this beauty was related to the very case he'd been put in charge of.

"In the wizarding world, it is not uncommon for the highest-ranking person of any group to automatically take charge."

"You're a wizard?" She sounded quite surprised.

Then again, he didn't look like the classic ones gallivanting about with airs of grandeur—and strong delusion. He didn't wear robes. He wasn't crazy about suits either.

"Don't tell anyone, but I am one of the strongest practitioners you will meet."

"And not conceited at all," was her sarcastic reply.

His lips quirked. "It's not conceited to state a verifiable truth. But I didn't come here to discuss my qualifications."

"Why are you here?"

"To take you to dinner."

She offered him a flat stare that said she didn't buy it. Smart woman. She wouldn't be easily swayed by flattery. He didn't mind a challenge.

"Your name came up as I was going over the files gathered related to the possible demon sightings—"

"No possible about it. I saw them with my own eyes."

"Which is why I wanted to speak with you."

"Why should I talk to you? Morfeus and his cronies made it very clear my opinion and aid weren't welcome."

"Morfeus is a moron. I am looking for the truth, and that involves speaking to everyone involved."

"Even a lowly witch?"

"I wouldn't call you lowly." Curvy, sexy, and distracting, yes.

"Don't say that around the TDCM."

"I will say what I please. The fact that some of my colleagues are narrow-minded doesn't mean we all are. Some of us recognize that witchcraft has its place in the world. It can also be quite useful. Most wizards won't admit it, but you are capable of magic they aren't."

Her nose scrunched up. "I find that hard to believe."

"All the races, humans included, have

something in their makeup. Call it an aptitude, or even more scientifically, a genome that changes how they do things, like magic. An elf has a greater ability to grow and heal things because of their affinity with nature. The shamans of the seas can do incredible feats with water."

"And what of human witches? What's our specialty?"

"You bring science and technology to your magic. Who do you think first invented potions?" He arched a brow.

"We did?" She frowned. "How come I've never heard this before?"

"Because then those who created the archaic rules would have to admit that witches deserve more respect."

"Did you get beaten up a lot at school?" she suddenly asked.

"No. Why?"

"Because you're spouting some awfully radical stuff. Mr…" she prompted him.

He smiled. "I am Alistair Fitzroy."

"*The* Fitzroy? The great archeologist and linguistic expert?"

"His son, actually. But striving for the same greatness." Not entirely true. He was already much more learned than Fitzroy senior; however, that kind of boast usually didn't go over well.

"Why does the TDCM need you?"

"To translate, of course."

At that, her nose wrinkled. "Translate what? As far as I know, the possessed spoke perfect English. I never heard any mention of incomprehensible speeches being babbled. They didn't leave any notes or manifestos."

"Ah, but that's where you're mistaken. It would appear you were not informed of what they found by the site of the Peabody crater."

"They found something?" Her eyes shone with curiosity. "What?"

"Join me for dinner if you want to find out."

"That's blackmail."

"Yes."

He could see she was tempted. So very, very tempted.

"Would it help if I said I'm making the TDCM pay for our very expensive meal?"

Her lips twitched. "It might."

"Then come. You choose the place."

"Why do you want to share information with me?"

"I told you before. I think it was shortsighted of them to boot you off the team. I'd like to rectify that."

"You want me to work with you." She said it with a note of incredulity.

"I do." Very closely, as a matter of fact.

She peeked down at her mauve outfit, the flouncy skirt and matching top bright. "I'm not really dressed to go out."

"Then we'll do something casual. Or, if you'd prefer, we can grab something and go back to my hotel room for"—privacy and a bed—"an uninterrupted chat."

She laughed. "Oh, that's a good one. Tease

me with information while trying to lure me to your room. I'm not that gullible."

"It was merely a suggestion. We can also stay somewhere public."

"Very public."

"If you insist."

"And I am following you in my car."

So many precautions, then again, given the rarity of women in this time, he could understand. Despite females of childbearing years being precious, their very rareness made them a commodity and a thing that others coveted.

She needn't worry with him. For all he found her absolutely delectable, he wasn't interested in her physical aspects.

Willow, the witch, had something else he wanted to get his hands on. He just had to get her to trust him enough so he could get closer and achieve his objective.

However, his cause took a major blow when he saw the thing she called a car.

His laughter was not appreciated.

Chapter Five

How dare he laugh at my Smart car?

I planted my hands on my hips—in a gesture wincingly reminiscent of my mother—and glared at him. "Stop laughing. This is not funny."

He pointed. "That is not a car."

"It is indeed a car. *My* car. And I don't appreciate your disparagement of what is a very environmentally friendly choice."

"It's a little can on four wheels. You would be better protected riding a bicycle with a helmet.

"A car isn't supposed to be a moving tank."

"I disagree."

"Let me guess, that's your truck?" I gestured to the military-grade Hummer parked out front.

"It is."

"Don't you think it's a little overboard?"

"A man in my position can't be too safe."

"You're killing the planet with your gas-guzzling beast." I inclined my head at his hulking metal machine.

"It won't be the release of carbon into the atmosphere that destroys the world."

"How would you know?"

"Because, according to the ancient texts I

studied, the coming apocalypse will."

"Apocalypse?" I snorted. "For a man of supposed intelligence, you need to stop reading the Bibles written in the past. We all know it was a time of suspicion where everything, even a priest farting, was a portent."

His lips twitched. "Don't mock the butterfly effect."

"Don't mock my car."

"I won't when you get a real one."

The man insulted me, yet I didn't get mad. I could hear the teasing undertone. If I didn't know better, I'd even say he flirted.

A wizard flirting with a witch? Unheard of. That was grounds for ostracism. There were strict rules about wizards and elves and other races muddying the bloodlines with humans. It totally made a girl want to run up to the most uptight wizard in a robe and lick his cheek while yelling, "Human cooties!"

It might be worth getting banished for life just to see their faces.

"Where are we going?" I asked. Because, despite his teasing, I did want to know what he'd found.

The great Fitzroy, or at least his probably paler imitation son, wouldn't have been called in by the TDCM over nothing.

What had Morfeus—that sly asshat—found that he hadn't shared?

"You choose the place," he said. "I'll follow and try not to squish you."

"The wheels on that thing are so jacked, I'd

probably slide under," I muttered, getting into my car. It was only slightly disconcerting to have him riding my tail—more like looming over it.

We ended up at a seafood and steak place where my dinner companion—not a date no matter how hard my nipples pointed through my bra—proceeded to devour an ungodly amount of food.

Now, it should be noted, I wasn't a lightweight when it came to eating. I had a healthy appetite, and my save-the-planet altruism didn't extend to meat. I needed protein in my world. And bacon.

But my ability to eat paled in comparison to his. He even put my brothers to shame.

"How many hours a day do you work out?" I asked, because he obviously did something to keep from turning into a giant butterball. Or was his handsome exterior an illusion?

"Intentional exercise?" He scoffed. "Only laggards have time for such things."

"Then how do you not turn into a blimp?"

He shrugged as he shoveled more food in. He swallowed before answering. "I feed my body the amount of fuel it needs."

"That's a lot of fuel," I noted.

"I am a very active man." The toothy smile made my stomach go into a gymnastic feat of flips that finished with a wet splash between my legs.

"You're also a very tight-lipped man. I came to dinner because you promised to give me information."

"And I will share, but first, I am curious

about the evening the Peabody house was eradicated. Could you tell me what happened?"

"I thought you read the reports."

"I did; however, a stale report can never replace the actual testimony of a witness. Sometimes speaking about something can jog the memory of details that were previously missed."

A valid point. "I'll tell you, but then I want to know what you found."

"Deal."

"It all began when a civilian went missing at the Peabody house."

Alistair nodded. "Brenda Whittaker. She was reported as missing, her vehicle located outside the Peabody home by a pack unit."

Pack unit meant Dale, the Alpha of a local Lycan group, and his buddies, Sebastian and Mike. They were werewolf shifters, and a pair of them, at least, worked with law enforcement.

I nodded. "It was Dale who called in the disappearance and the suspicious appearance of the Peabody house."

"Morfeus assembled a team to check on it."

"Morfeus assembled his buddies to check it out," I corrected. "Dale happened to call me and let me in on what was happening."

"And how did Dale find out?"

"Police dispatch got called. Apparently, the neighbors got suspicious about the place. It went from looking pristine and perfect to falling-down decrepit."

His intent gaze and apparent genuine interest made it easy to talk to him. He didn't display any of the mockery or give any of the insults I'd gotten used to. "The file didn't have any images to show the condition of the home. Can you elaborate on what the neighbors saw?"

"I can't give you a basis for comparison. That night was the first time I'd visited the Peabody home in person. So I have no idea what it looked like before. All I know is that when I pulled up, it appeared as if the yard hadn't been tended in years. The grass was dead and yellow. The house itself had peeling paint and curled roof tiles. If I'd not seen pictures of it after the minor fire—"

"—a fire Peabody set."

"Yes. He wanted to burn down the house and get rid of the thing possessing it. But the damage from the fire was minor. Just a singed porch, apparently."

Alistair leaned back and appeared thoughtful. "Interesting. Whatever problem occurred within the house caused it to alter its appearance. A force that knew enough to project a glamour showing that nothing was awry while it siphoned off the energy of the home."

"The energy?" I frowned at him. "What do you mean?" I hated asking, but as Mother said, you only learned by asking questions.

"Everything has energy."

"I thought that only applied to living things."

"Were the materials of a home not once living? The wood, the fabrics, everything but stone, is harvested, and while not as potent as when alive, the lingering energy is there for consumption."

"What you're saying is that whatever infested the house ate it." It sounded dumb to say aloud, yet he nodded his head.

"It used some of the energy it imbibed to camouflage its actions."

The question I had was, "Did it do so as an automatic defense mechanism, or because of conscious thought?"

He shrugged. "A bit of both, I'd wager. Survival is always one of the prime directives of any species. Once the predator took root, its first order of business was to protect itself."

"And then what?"

He shrugged. "Conquer using the observed possession techniques. Grow. I would imagine, had it been left unchecked, it would have spread past its current boundary into adjacent homes. Preparing for the event."

"Event? Are you talking full-scale invasion? Via some kind of dimensional portal in that house?" Saying it aloud didn't make it sound any more real. "That's nuts."

"Do you have a better explanation?" His blue eyes met mine, steady and serious. "Look at the evidence. We have a sudden infestation of…let's call them parasites, coming into the world, attached to hosts. How are they getting here?"

"They could have been in hiding all this time like the rest of the supers."

His brow arched. "Do you really believe these bloodthirsty creatures have been amongst us all this time, behaving?" His sarcasm curled around the words.

"They do seem kind of out of control." At least the ones I'd met. "But that doesn't make them dimension-jumping creatures. Could be some land developer dug in the wrong spot and freed them from some long-lost cavern?"

He gaped at me, incredulous at my logic obviously—and courtesy of all the horror movies I'd watched as a kid. As a witch, I felt it was my duty to prepare myself for any possibility.

"They did not crawl out of a cave. They come from another dimension. A different world."

"Says you."

"Says the evidence."

Either he lied, or the demons weren't from here. But if that were the case, how did we stop them from infiltrating?

"How do we stop them?"

"By finding the holes and sealing them."

"Blowing up more houses. Got it." Except I didn't get it. Who knew to destroy the Peabody house? "So I guess we watch for news of haunted houses and people going a little batty. Then we swoop in and slam it into the ground."

"It won't always be that noticeable. Keep in mind, the rips and the entities coming through them are in survival mode. They're hiding."

"Which makes me wonder, how come we never detected the glamour?" I leaned forward. "Surely it emitted some kind of magical frequency."

"Not all magic is detectable."

"No. However, something of this

magnitude, and cast on an inanimate object, should have created some kind of vibration on an esoteric level," I prodded. I should have seen something. Anyone with magic should have, yet not one person, not even I, saw a haze in the air.

"You're right. Usually, there would be some kind of trace. Yet no one has admitted to seeing anything. So either everyone who visited that home is incompetent, or they willfully lied."

"Or the magic was too subtle," I added. "Which raises an interesting question. Can you hide magic with magic?"

"Does it matter?"

Yes, actually. If the portals to this other realm siphoned energy and, as part of their nature, hid, then it was one thing. But what if it wasn't the rip doing the hiding? What if it was sly and intentional?

I'd assumed, as had others thus far, that the demons were mindless, murderous creatures, but what if they were something more than that? What if they were intelligent?

I must have shivered because he asked, "Are you cold?"

"I'm fine." Fine, but not ready to speak aloud my theory about smart demons. Bad enough we discussed interdimensional rips in time and space. "We seem to have gotten off track. You were asking about the house. I pulled up, and I remember it was dark. Very dark. The streetlights weren't working." It could only mean bad things. I didn't need a movie to tell me that.

"So how could you see?" he asked.

"The headlights on my car showed me how wrecked the front yard was." The twin beams added a surreal effect to the dead lawn, especially where it bordered the lush green grass of its neighbor. "I remember getting out and seeing Morfeus on the sidewalk." My brow wrinkled. I'd seen him standing there and turning to face the house because the door was opening. But who came out?

We were all outside at that point. I, Morfeus, and his crew, even Brenda and her werewolves were safely outside. So who did that leave?

We never did recover a body for Peabody's wife.

"You just thought of something," Alistair prodded.

It startled me that he'd guessed so accurately. I caught his gaze and couldn't look away.

What mesmerizing blue eyes he had, with a hint of something in the center of them.

I found myself speaking without even realizing it. "There was someone in the house."

"Who?"

"I—I—" I felt like I knew the answer. It was right there, hiding behind some cobwebs in my mind, but no matter how I tried to brush them aside, I came up empty-handed.

"Was it male? Female? Something else?"

I shook my head. "I don't know. I remember the front door opening. Red." Redder than my own hair. "And a feeling of..." Skin prickling, ozone in the air, a hushed anticipation and stomach-clenching fear. "Danger."

"Danger from what?"

"I don't know. Everything goes fuzzy after that." As if someone had thrown a blanket over my memories. "The next thing I know, I'm standing on the sidewalk—"

"In the same place?"

A gnawing of my lower lip helped me concentrate. "No, actually. I was closer to the house, what was left of it. There was smoke billowing, and flames. Such pretty blue flames."

"Blue?"

"Yes, blue, which means they were magically induced. But none of us recall doing it. And I'll be honest, I don't think Morfeus has the kind of power it takes to fuel blue flames of that magnitude." Most wizards could create fire, regular orange flames, the kind that singed and burned. However, the blue kind that eradicated not only a house but also the very stone within it, could also eliminate magic.

"Who was there at that point?"

"Still the same people. Brenda and the wolf pack. All three of them. Morfeus and his guys— two of them—were there, too; although they looked a little worse for wear."

"Did you all suffer the time lapse?"

"Yes, but I didn't know it at the time. Initially, I didn't even realize I'd lost minutes. Everything was so chaotic, especially once the firemen arrived." While hunky, they'd served no practical purpose. A magical fire couldn't be put out by conventional means.

"Did you stick around?"

"Only for a few minutes. I didn't want to get caught up by human authorities. So I employed a tiny spell of look-away, hopped in my car, and left."

"Alone."

"Yeah, alone. Except for my cat."

"You brought your cat with you to a scene of possible demonic activity?" He arched a brow.

"I'm a witch. We need familiars."

"Most don't carry them around."

"True, but Whiskers is just a kitten. I'd adopted him earlier that day and hadn't yet gotten him home." My cute little baby furball. I recalled being so glad he'd remained safe in my car that night.

"Back to the house and the door that opened."

"I already told you, I don't remember anything. And I've given you enough." I leaned back in my seat and crossed my arms. "Your turn to spill something."

"What would you like to know?"

"Everything," was my blunt reply.

"A broad request. Perhaps you could fine-tune it."

"What's the newest thing to come in on the demon situation?"

"I received the complete autopsy results on Peabody this afternoon."

My sources sucked; either that or I needed to up my bribes. "And what did the report say?" I leaned forward.

"Nothing. Whatever possessed him left no physiological trace."

"What of a magical one?"

He shrugged. "None that the examining elders could find. But they are still running tests. A pity we didn't get him in a lab before he expired. We might have seen more."

"Didn't the elders"—elven wizards so old that people just fawned over them wherever they went—"visit him while he was in the sanatorium?"

"As if they'd stoop to visiting a Lycan-run facility." Alistair rolled his eyes.

I could understand his mockery. The fights between the species were, at times, ridiculous, and in this case, misplaced.

The Lycium Institute had been created by the Lycan clans to deal with natural-born werewolves who couldn't handle their altered state. It wasn't easy for someone born and raised as a human to suddenly discover his never-before-met daddy had left him a little genetic surprise.

Then there were those who just went crazy. Since they couldn't exactly blend in with the human patients, they needed a special place to go where they wouldn't automatically be killed.

When they discovered that Peabody had issues, they'd sent him to Lycium since they were the best equipped to handle him. Except no one anticipated the level of crazy they'd have to deal with.

"I went to see him once before he died." Before he'd turned catatonic.

"Peabody?" Alistair stopped drumming his fingers. "Did he say anything?"

He had, but it was more how I felt when in his presence that stuck with me. It still made me shiver to remember the man. The thing inside him looking out of his eyes.

I'd had to jump through hoops just to get in.

Upon arriving at the institute, the attending doctor had taken one look at my flame-red hair and said, "Oh, hell no. No red allowed."

Having been discriminated against before because of my looks and subjected to profiling like the person who assumed I had a wicked temper—totally true—I wasn't completely shocked by the blatant rejection. Usually, they at least pretended to hide it.

While not hurt by the doctor's rebuff, I had wavered on the side of insulted. "There is nothing wrong with red hair. As a matter of fact, did you know redheaded people tend to score higher on the intelligence meters?" I admit I made that up. The actual truth of the claim was still a mystery I didn't bother looking up. Why, when I personally knew it for a fact?

The doctor had looked apologetic. "Love the hair, but you can't see Peabody with it showing." It was interesting to note that Frank, as stated on the tag, wore a lovely wig in a shade of platinum, brilliant blue eyeshadow, and a peach-hued gloss. He also bore a full beard.

At the time, I remembered thinking I needed to up my game since Frank's phone kept pinging, the brief flashes of messages distracting with their, *Hey, hottie. See you tonight. Wear that little dress.*

Frank was getting more action than I was.

But I wasn't there to find a man—that was reserved for Sunday night dinner at my parents' house where my mom tried to set me up with every single guy she ran into.

My mother appeared quite perturbed that her only daughter hadn't managed to settle down and pop out a handful of kids already.

Apparently, I needed to do my part. I didn't see why she couldn't bug my brothers about ensuring the continuity of our family name.

But, anyhow, Frank—who smelled more expensive than my Dove soap—proceeded to explain how the color red set Peabody off.

Not exactly eager to tease a demon-bull, I borrowed a hooded sweater from him and raised it over my head.

My pride and glory was hidden, and I wasn't sure how I felt about that. Shouldn't it be my choice what I hid from the world?

A fear of scalping by a crazy man made the decision for me.

Due to his violent outbursts, they'd restricted Peabody to his room, a big, padded one.

When I walked in, he was on the ceiling.

Not hanging from it, but literally on the ceiling, hanging upside down, clinging to it crablike.

Kind of freaky, especially since it was happening for real and not in a movie.

Staring up at him, I really questioned my decision to go see him.

Why did you go? What did you hope to find out?

The questions slightly jarred my recollection. Who was that talking to me? Seeing into my mind?

Shhhh. It's no one. Keep talking.

Don't you mean remembering? Remembering how Peabody's head had canted at an unnatural angle. How his eyes, the whites of them gone, were black, bottomless pits, and in their depths...

Shiver.

I didn't like to attribute good or evil to things. Not without knowing them at least, but that thing, and it was a *thing* at that point, no person left inside, it screamed one absolute.

Evil.

If I'd had a crossbow, I would have probably shot him with it.

And then found a sword to take off its head.

As it was, I raised my hands to cast a protective shield when it spoke.

What did it say?

The teasing words had emerged on a low-timbered hiss. "*If it isn't the witch come to say hello. Did no one warn you what a lovely snack you make?*"

The comparison to food and me particularly bothered. I knew demons liked witches. But Peabody, as yet, hadn't fully changed. For some reason, his demon was stuck inside.

Why do you think he was stuck?

Because he'd not yet eaten enough witches.

I think the hunger of his demon was what made Peabody snap. He'd been contained before he could fully possess his body.

He was stuck in between states. Not man, not beast.

And it hungered.

What else did it say?

The insistent questioning snapped me out of the fugue state I was in.

I glared at the man across the table. "What the hell do you think you're doing?"

"Whatever do you mean?"

The man aimed for innocence, but I knew better. I saw right through it. "I mean, what the fuck are you doing compelling me to share my memories?"

For a moment, I thought he'd deny it again.

"I needed to find out certain things."

"Why not just ask? I have been telling you everything I know."

"Telling me what you think you remember you mean. I need more than that."

"That doesn't give you the right to muck around with my head." I glared.

"Actually, the High Council has given me wide leeway in dealing with this matter. I don't have time to play games, Willow. I am only here for one reason."

"To mind-fuck me?" I'd stopped being nice the moment I realized what he'd done.

"These are grave times. If your world—"

"'Don't you mean *our* world?"

Finally, he looked agitated. "Can you stop

speaking for a moment while I explain?"

"No. Because you should have explained before you laid a whammy on me." Standing, I made sure to look as angry as my red roots could manage when I spat, "Good luck finding the demon. Better make it sooner rather than later, though, because, while you wizards are dicking around, you all seem to forget something. Demons don't just enjoy witch blood."

And with that, I stomped off.

Chapter Six

Such a temper.

Alistair stared musingly after Willow. She appeared royally peeved. With good reason.

She'd caught him playing with her mind. Yet she shouldn't have. Alistair was good at what he did.

Extracting information took a certain finesse. A subject noticing and rebuffing his methods of gathering information was unheard of.

Very intriguing.

Not fascinating enough to follow tonight, though. Not with the text he'd received.

Might be a live one in the warehouse district.

A live demon? Most excellent. It was time they found one to question.

Send the coordinates to my phone, he commanded via text.

Shall I send backup?

Not necessary. I've got it covered. Let them assume he'd called some in. Assume incorrectly, he should add. Alistair had no need of aid. More people would just get in his way.

It didn't take long in his truck—which had an impressive ability to get people to move out of his way—before he'd made it to the coordinates on his phone.

Back in the warehouse district. He wondered for a moment if he'd end up back at Willow's place of work.

Is the demon hunting her? While he didn't sense strong magic from her, those hungry beasts wouldn't care. Any magic would do.

That would suck. While he didn't mix business and pleasure, she almost tempted him enough to make an exception.

He drove past her warehouse, which was lit all around with bright, UV-grade lights. Which was less for the vampires who really didn't care about light of any kind than for the tunnelpfiefer, mole-like creatures that only emerged at night and liked to borrow things.

The tunnelpfiefer called it borrowing; human laws labeled it stealing. Tensions were running high inside the cities that hadn't yet run them out.

Bleeding heart liberals said they didn't mean any harm. They'd keep repeating that until a tunnelpfiefer snuck into their house and stole their baby.

Experience changed many a person's mind.

Alistair reached the end of the road where the coordinates led and drove past the dark building before parking. He'd work his way back, but first, a few preparations.

Exiting his truck, Alistair rounded to the rear of it and opened the hatch. Within sat a box, a special one that only he could open.

The sealed crate stank of magic the moment

he unsealed it. Various articles filled it: wands—for siphoning power to be used at a later date—a few empty potion flasks—*I really should get those refilled*—some clothing he'd bought off the underground, esoteric market...

What use did a man have for used garments? Watch and learn.

Alistair pulled out a femininely scented jacket reeking of witch. Amazing how much humans imprinted the things they touched. Even some wizards were lax about guarding their true selves.

He shut the lid to his box of toys and tossed the coat a few yards from him. Then he hunched down to wait.

Alistair knew quite a few things about demons—and the hunting of them.

Such as the fact that newer ones couldn't sift scents to detect whether something was living or just a smelly piece of clothing.

The body rushed from the shadows and past the discarded jacket before stopping and turning with a confused look. It crouched down and sniffed. While it was distracted, Alistair flowed forward and shot out a fist, clocking it.

A few punches past a slobbering mouth, the teeth barely pointed, and a sweep of the ankles that sent the misshapen thing to the ground, and Alistair could pin it.

He knelt on the newly minted demon's chest, a flabby human one, the host being an uninspiring sort with patchy blond hair that had lost its comb-over, pasty, pockmarked skin, and beady eyes.

"You didn't exactly choose a pleasant host, did you?" Then again, demons that wished to escape their realm didn't have much choice. The rips appeared and disappeared without notice. Sometimes lasting days. Other times, only hours.

A demon who wanted to escape couldn't afford to be picky about a host. It sent out its essence to the first viable body it found. Then, it went hunting.

The thing opened its mouth and made a noise, the stench of its breath appalling.

Alistair parted his lips and...laughed. "You do realize that would only be frightening to children? And only young ones at that."

The voice croaked, "I shall feast on your blood. Grind your bones."

"First, you'd have to actually extricate yourself. You're weak."

"Not for long."

It would only take a few magical feedings for the demon to be able to pull his full self over onto the Earth side. Even then, it would have to keep feeding to maintain the tether and avoid the poisonous atmosphere.

"How did you get here? Where is the portal?"

The thing cackled. "There are many doorways now. The cracks between the worlds are widening. We are spilling in."

"I know that already. I want to know where *you* came in." The Peabody location had been shut, but there were other spots that required investigation.

"Where the sun rises over the shining building."

"That describes half of downtown." Alistair sighed. "But it's a start. Did you come here by accident or intent?"

"I am the harbinger of death."

Eye-rolling-worthy declaration. "Who sent you?"

"The King of Terrible Countenance."

"Does your king have a name?" Because the demons didn't have just one lord.

"He has many names, for he is the Son of Perdition, the Mighty Conqueror."

"In other words, another wannabe destroyer. Have you not all learned your lesson? Do you not recall the world you already destroyed?" The demon realm used to be a place of beauty. Then, it was invaded.

Unless stopped, Earth would suffer the same fate.

"We shall conquer. Blood will fill the streets. Victory for the king."

Mindless madness. Alistair leaned close and whispered, "Would you die for your king?"

A hint of pride entered the demon's gaze, and a wide, toothy grin pulled his bloodless lips. "The legion is ready to die for its king."

Alistair smiled, and a tendril of smoke curled.

"You are indeed legion and, in time of need, expendable. Rejoice, minion of chaos, for they will recycle your name to the next warrior in line," he promised.

Then Alistair wrung the demon's neck.

Chapter Seven

My phone began to chirp, and I glared at it on my nightstand. No good ever came from answering the phone this late—and by late, I meant ten p.m. Good girls, even witches, went to bed early.

The number on the screen wasn't familiar, yet I answered because, hey, maybe I'd get a heavy breather or someone asking what I was wearing. I wouldn't mind taking out my frustration on someone, and a perv would suit that role nicely.

Except when I answered, "Who is it?" a velvety smooth voice replied.

"I hope I'm not disturbing you."

He totally was, but not by calling. The fact that Fitzroy existed disturbed me. The fact that he'd managed to slip past my defenses almost unnoticed bothered me. The way my body reacted to just the sound of his voice pissed me off.

"What do you want?"

"To offer an apology."

"Does it include copious amounts of chocolate?"

"Uh, no."

"Then it's just words."

I hung up.

Held on to my phone and stared at it.

Sure enough, it rang. I stared and didn't answer.

One ring. Two. Three. Just before voicemail, I accepted with a sigh—that I hoped didn't relay any of my tingling excitement.

"You're vexing me."

Good. "I don't want to talk to you."

"Before you hang up, I might not have chocolate, but I do have something else to tempt."

Dammit. I'd forgotten about the bribe he'd used to drag me to dinner. "You mean that thing you never showed me."

"You rushed off before I could. I still want to show you."

The way he said that imbued the words with all kinds of extra meaning. "Fine. Bring it by my office tomorrow."

"I'm afraid the bureau won't let me bring it out of their lockup. You'll have to come to the TDCM to view it."

The very thought of dealing with the arrogant pricks there made me want to say, "no way." However, he'd piqued my interest. "Let me know what time."

"How about after the autopsy?"

That word had me sitting up straighter in bed. "Who died?" Had another witch been eviscerated and no one told me?

"I caught a demon."

"And killed it?" I'd been hoping for another live one. One like Peabody, capable of speech. There were so many questions to ask, and corpses, even reanimated ones, weren't much for conversation.

"I'm sorry, perhaps I should have let it kill me instead." Such sarcasm.

I kind of enjoyed it.

"Where did you find it?" I asked.

"How about we discuss this in the morning. Say, eight a.m. Meet you at the morgue."

"I am assuming you mean the TDCM morgue and not the human one."

"Don't state the obvious. We both know you're smarter than that."

A backhanded compliment that made me blush.

"I'll be there." How far would the ass-kissing go? "Don't forget to bring coffee. And donuts." I hung up the phone—before I could ask him to say something dirty—and tapped my chin.

Morning seemed both too soon and too far. I didn't know if I could wait that long.

Impatience wanted me to meet with Alistair now, this very minute.

And not because of the demon case.

From the moment I answered, I'd found myself tingling. Wanting.

What is wrong with me? I should have told him no freaking way, not after what he'd pulled with the mind control thing, but...I couldn't afford to push him away. I couldn't let my personal feelings—of which annoyance played a strong part—get in the way of what was good for my coven. I needed to know more about demons, and Alistair offered me the best chance.

That was why I'd agreed to meet him, and

despite the excitement and fluttery feeling I felt—mostly between my legs—I lied to myself. I was excited about the prospect of dissecting a demon body and really didn't care if I saw Fitzroy.

One thing I would give him credit for was bringing me in on the autopsy. Apparently, Alistair meant what he'd said about exploring all avenues and using every resource he had. I wasn't sure how I felt about being one of those resources. He'd mentioned witches had different magic than wizards. He was right. We did do things differently, which meant I'd be bringing some of my tools to the autopsy.

Whether or not the person in charge of dissecting allowed me to use them remained to be seen. Would Alistair intervene if necessary?

Even if he didn't, I'd take what I could get. I'd gotten my foot back into the demon investigation. Sure, a dead body wasn't the most exciting thing in the grand scheme of things, but curiosity made me wonder if my potions could see something the la-di-da wizards didn't.

Nothing, however, would happen until the morning.

Hours from now.

Why wait? The case demanded urgency, yet I didn't argue with the timeframe when I spoke to Alistair. I could have, yet I hadn't because there was no way I was leaving my house at night alone. These were dangerous times for witches on their own.

It was dangerous for kitties, too. Slipping out of my bed, I once again peeked out the window, hoping for a glimpse of my cat, barely more than a kitten. And a dumbass.

We hadn't yet completed our bond as witch and familiar. I'd only recently acquired Whiskers. I'd found him, my orange stray, by chance, right around the time of the Peabody incident. The timing couldn't have been better.

I'd lost Percy, my previous cat, the one who'd seen me through my very first spell at the age of nine, a few months before. He'd lived a long life, my Percy. Seen me screw up more than I liked to admit.

As I got older and more comfortable in my magical skills, I didn't use Percy as much. However, I'd not realized how much I would miss having a pet until he was gone.

The heartache of his loss made me swear to live without. Then Whiskers came into my life with a soft meow.

Where are you, furball? Since getting him, he'd never spent the night outside, preferring to snuggle under the blankets against my lower back. All good and great until he started massaging with his claws.

He'd escaped outside on me a few times, but he hadn't gone far. This time, however, he'd raced for the fence, climbed it, and took off.

Some people would have gone tearing after him. I knew better. Cats were strong-willed, independent creatures. He'd come back when he was good and ready.

But that didn't mean I wouldn't try and tempt him.

I threw on a robe and some slippers before

heading to the kitchen. The food bowl sat still full of kibble. I opened the sliding back door a crack. Only a sliver that I could easily slam shut. I shook the food bowl, rattling the dry nibbles within.

Nothing.

Slamming the door shut, I went for the bigger guns. I cracked open a fresh can of tuna and tossed it onto the deck. Maybe the strong smell would draw him.

Minutes later, and still nothing. My back porch light lit the entire tiny deck, and I didn't even see a shadow twitch.

I stuck my head out the door and made ridiculous kissy noises.

Go to bed.

Whiskers would come home when he was damned well ready.

But he's a baby.

What if he was stuck? I ventured outside. Slowly, mind you. I knew how those other witches had lost their lives. Looking for their damned cat, that's how.

But still, I couldn't let the possibility that my feline had been taken over by a demon stop me from caring. Whiskers was just a baby, which was why I crept into the yard, wand in hand, incantation ready to fly.

The smell struck me first. A kind of rotten egg scent with a hint of something burning.

The dewy, green grass cushioned my slippered feet as I stepped onto it, the shadows not so deep in my fenced yard. The moon globes I'd placed every two feet kept the worst at bay.

My gaze darted around, taking in details, like my outdoor clock, the hands at a quarter to eleven. Not the witching hour, as some would call it, but close enough to make me nervous.

Especially when I saw it over by the vegetable garden.

No mistaking the burn marks in my grass.

I bolted back to the safety of the house, slammed the door shut, grabbed a phone, and dialed.

"Psychic Network, you need it, we know it," said the bored male who answered.

"This is a call for the TDCM," I stated.

"Wrong number."

I held in a sigh. The wizards and their games. What was this month's secret phrase? Oh, yes. "I love the smell of napalm in the morning." Whoever had submitted that one was an old movie buff.

Immediately, the tone of his voice changed. "How can I help you, ma'am?"

"I'd like to report a theft."

"Ma'am, this line is for serious magical emergencies. Theft and other petty crimes should be called in to the regular police."

"Not a normal kind of theft."

"Was it a magical artifact? Is it dangerous?"

"Not exactly. It's my cat."

"We don't deal with lost pets."

"Well, you'd better this time because I am fairly certain a demon stole my kitty."

"Demon?" He snorted. "Why would you think that?"

Because of the clawed paw prints singed into my lawn. "Just trust me when I say there was a demon in my yard."

"Why would a demon be in your yard?"

"Because I'm a witch, you moron. You know what? I am just going to call the guy in charge." Because, hello, I knew him.

Of course, the one thing I'd not planned on when calling was Alistair actually showing up at my place.

It was only as I opened the door, my robe gaping open, that I realized what I wore.

Hello Kitty onesie pajamas.

And he noticed.

Chapter Eight

"You can stop snickering anytime now," Willow growled, her face a scowl of annoyance.

Yet how could he stop his mirth? A grown woman wearing a cartoon pajama that would be more suitable for a baby? Too much.

"How do you use the washroom in one of those?" he asked. It seemed rather complicated as outfits went.

Turning to give him a view of her rear—where he noticed a square flap—she wiggled her butt. "Two Velcro snaps and I'm good to go."

Surely, she didn't mean…he realized how it would look, the square of fabric pulling away, revealing an opening through which only her posterior would emerge.

Obscenely interesting.

Also very distracting.

Diverting his gaze, he stared at her head. "Where did you see the demon?" Time to get back on track and business.

"I didn't see a demon."

"But your text said demon at my house."

"Was. He's gone now. It's probably easier if I show you. Follow me." She led the way through her small house to a sliding glass door at the back.

She stepped through, and Alistair smelled it immediately.

His gaze honed in on the scorch marks on the ground. They started mid-yard and marched to the fence. He followed and noted the burn marks on the tops of the boards.

He whirled on her. "Why were you outside? You know it's dangerous for your kind at night." She knew of the demon problem, why would she risk herself?

"I was looking for my cat."

No point in chastising her about her reason. He knew how attached witches were to their felines. "Did you find it?"

"No, because the demon took it."

"How can you tell? Perhaps it ran off, frightened."

That earned him a dirty look. "Whiskers doesn't get scared. And I know a demon took him because look at what he crushed into the ground."

She jabbed her finger toward a perfect imprint, six-toed, pressed into the charred lawn. "A collar. Whiskers' collar."

"Perhaps he slipped it off."

"Or maybe the most obvious thing is fact: the demon took him."

"Better the cat than you."

The punch to his arm was harder than he'd have expected. He tossed her a startled look and got treated to a harangue.

"Don't you dare make light of this. Whiskers is my baby. We need to find him."

"Don't you mean find the demon?"

"Find the demon, and you probably find my kitten."

Digested and left as excrement wherever the thing nested. Best not to mention that quite yet.

"How do you suggest we follow this demon when we don't even know what it looks like?" he asked, rising from his crouch to eye the fence he really didn't want to climb. The slacks he wore were for looking sleek, not stretching.

"How hard can it be? You're the wizard. Surely, you have a spell."

"You're a witch, and I don't see you waving your wand and casting," he retorted. Although she did have a valid point. Some trackers could enhance the trail of their quarry with magic, strengthening the scent or, in some cases, even illuminating their steps for a short time.

But those weren't demons. They were too cunning to be tracked so easily.

"I can only brew something up if I've got a trace of the thing I'm looking for. Hair, skin, fingernail."

"Burnt footprint won't work?" he asked, pointing.

"Not unless he left blood behind. This is useless. You're useless." She flung her hands in annoyance and stalked back into her home.

He spent a moment staring at the burnt prints. Large steps. Upper-caste demon. Stalking the witch?

He didn't like that. There weren't many reasons for a demon to be in her yard. The most obvious one was dinner.

Alistair followed the witch, only to find the sliding glass door locked. He rattled it then pounded.

"Let me in."

She appeared on the other side of the glass and shook her head. "You can go now. We're obviously not going to find my cat."

I can go? Did she seriously think she could dismiss him?

"We need to discuss what the appearance of a demon means."

"I am not a complete idiot. I know what it means. I'm next on its menu."

"You need to take precautions."

"You're right, I do, and yet you're wasting my time yapping when I could be casting."

She turned her back on him and, with a wave of her hand, tugged the curtain shut.

He stared at it.

Then laughed.

Game on, witch. Game on.

Chapter Nine

Having spent the night tracing every protective rune I could think of on every windowsill, door, crack, or hole in my house, I was understandably tired.

One might even say I was feeling downright bitchy when my doorbell rang at the ungodly hour of seven a.m. the following day.

I shoved my head under a pillow and ignored it.

The person was obviously an asshole since they rang it again.

And again.

And again.

They also knocked.

"Dammit it all to hell," I yelled as I stalked to the door, my hair a wild, red mess, my onesie pajama exchanged for something cooler that only barely covered the tops of my thighs. And, no, I didn't change it in case a certain wizard popped by again.

Cough. Liar. My own mind mocked me.

A more cautious woman would have asked who banged at the door. I mean, there was a demon roaming the neighborhood, after all, but it was daylight, and I had enough annoyance coursing through me to probably handle a few of them this morning.

I flung open the door with a snarled, "Run before I rip your hand off."

"But I come bearing coffee."

I blinked at Kal. Why was my assistant on my front step? "What are you doing here?"

"First, a sip of coffee."

Kal never dropped by first thing in the morning armed with caffeine. This couldn't be good. I grabbed the cardboard cup and sipped. Pure black coffee. Nothing to sweeten or dilute the flavor.

It went down smoothly, as did the donut Kal shoved at me. Whatever he had to relate wasn't good. He only resorted to feeding me when he knew my day was about to go to shit.

Braced, I eyed him. "You've fed the beast. Now, spill."

His purple-rimmed glasses slid down his nose, and Kal shoved them back up the bridge. "So, the alarm company beeped me last night."

"You? How come they didn't call me?" I frowned. Given I paid their damned invoice every month, you'd think they'd have the courtesy to list me as their main contact.

"They called me because you are the coven leader. As the boss, you shouldn't be called every single time a rat trips the motion detector."

"That doesn't happen."

"Yeah, it does. About once a week on average."

"So you've been getting the calls?" That

wasn't the most awful thing Kal could have done. Although he could have told me.

Then again, if he had, I'd have probably told him not to do it. He was right. I did take on too much responsibility.

"So why did they ding you? Were there teenagers spraying graffiti again?" Their obscene artwork was what had led to me hire the company in the first place. Getting the walls clean—because the city didn't care who wrote *Witches suck dick*—was more expensive than expected.

"Don't freak out."

The longer Kal stalled, the worse I knew it was going to be.

"I will freak out if I want. It's my prerogative!"

"We kind of had a break-in last night."

"Did they steal our stash?" And by stash, I didn't mean drugs. We had more valuable stuff than that. We had a locked vault of spell ingredients, some of them very rare. Unicorn horn, mermaid toenails—which were impossible to get since most chose to never leave the tail or the sea.

"The vault is untouched, but everything else…" Kal hesitated before saying in a rush, "Everything else was trashed."

I might have let out an expletive that would have gotten my mouth washed out with soap as a child—an entire bar, maybe two, it was so profane.

"Do we know who did it?" I muttered when I'd calmed down enough to only pace rather than throw fireballs at my walls. My house didn't deserve to be punished because of hoodlums.

"Not who. What."

I paused and pivoted, fixing my assistant with a stare. "Talk faster, Kal, or you'll be in the unemployment line for dragging this out." I wouldn't actually fire him, he was too damned efficient, but this slow meting of information was too much.

"The TDCM hasn't officially ruled on it—"

"What!" I might have screamed. "They're involved?"

"—but all indications point to it being a demon."

A freaking demon had destroyed my warehouse.

But that wasn't the worst of it.

"The coven records are missing."

It took a moment for that to filter. Because, in my mind, demons were dumb animals. What use would they have for my records?

Yet, just last night, hadn't I wondered, what if they weren't stupid? What if demons could read? If that was the case then...

"Oh my God, they have the address of every single witch in the city."

We were all in danger.

Immediately, I went into action. Luckily, I kept a backup of all coven records in a fireproof and thief-proof box in my house. We had to contact them as soon as possible and get them somewhere safe.

Only once I'd set up Kal at my place, my dining room the new temporary headquarters, did I get dressed and ready to go. He had a lot of calls to make while I found out what the hell was going on.

As I raced to the warehouse district, I noted the time. Quarter after eight. I'd missed my meeting with Alistair for the autopsy. If I was even still invited. Hell, for all I knew, he was the one overseeing the investigation on the attack at my warehouse.

I can't believe they hit my coven office. The deliberate attack left me chilled.

The demons had raised the stakes. Now it wasn't only my life in danger, but also everyone who'd come in contact with the coven. Witches not just in my city and the states surrounding it, but contacts from across the country—the globe—as well.

So many people. Innocents. Many with barely enough magic to imbue a potion with luck.

All possible victims if I didn't do something.

But what? What could I do to stop these creatures?

Especially since I couldn't even get the young idiot guarding the perimeter to my place to let me in.

"This area is off-limits."

Don't kill him. Don't kill him.

A light breeze tugged at my red hair as my nails dug into my palms. "I'm part of the demon taskforce."

"You're not a wizard." He sneered. "Only authorized personnel can enter."

"I am the coven leader. This is my building." I fought not to raise my voice. Losing my temper wouldn't help me.

"This property is now under the care of the TDCM. Move back."

No "please." No, "hey let's get you talking to someone in charge."

Just an asshole about to get his face rearranged. Because, like it or not, I was going in.

Chapter Ten

The phone in Alistair's pocket kept buzzing, and he ignored it. It hadn't stopped since he took over for Morfeus.

People nagging him. Inviting him to dinner. To parties. To meet their daughters. All of them sycophants looking to curry favor.

It irritated.

Why couldn't they be more like Willow, who locked him out and refused to deal with him?

A woman who'd spent the night working on reinforcing the spells protecting her house. He should know. He'd watched over her from a nearby rooftop. Ensuring her safety, despite not understanding his need to do so.

Since when do I protect strangers? Since when did he care?

She was just a witch. A nobody. Yet that didn't stop him from finding a spot to spy on her.

He contented himself with the argument that the demon might return and need to be dealt with. *I'm no hero.* A hero wouldn't do the things he'd done. Spilled so much blood.

And he'd spill more. Alistair wasn't a male to shy away from necessity.

He'd perched like a watching gargoyle,

keeping a sharp eye out for attack until the last of her lights went off, and she finally got some rest.

Only when the dawn cracked the horizon did he finally relent. Demons didn't like sunlight. It dried out their usually moist skin and hurt the sensitive membrane over their eyes.

With his unusual protection endeavor over for the moment, he hastened to Fairy Fingers, the TDCM science lab. He'd entrusted the demon body to them and wanted to be on hand to ensure that they didn't proceed until Willow had joined him.

He had, after all, killed it just for her.

Some men courted women with flowers and jewels. He gave the witch a body.

Is that what I'm doing? Courting her?

It stunned him to realize that he had no other reason to act as he had.

I want her trust, so she'll work with me.

Why? He didn't need a witch on his side. Didn't need anyone, actually.

His phone buzzed again in his pocket. Since he drove, he ignored it. The ability for people to bother him anywhere, anytime was one he could do without. Whoever thought it a good idea to make phones portable should be shot.

The building housing the secret TDCM lab and morgue, titled an odd Fairy Fingers, bustled with activity, unlike the headquarters that always oozed a certain quiet calm. Having never been here before, Alistair didn't realize it was unusual for this hour until the receptionist, a silver-haired woman with peach-colored lips and brilliant emerald eyes exclaimed, "Sir, why are you here instead of at the scene of the crime?"

"What are you talking about?"

"Our office has been trying to contact you. The team is at the site of a possible demon incident."

"Where?"

"Didn't you receive our text?"

No, because he'd turned his cell to silent while keeping watch over the witch and then ignored it because it annoyed him. He preferred to work alone.

Whipping out his phone, he quickly scrolled through the missed calls and messages. But it was the address of the demon attack that made his blood run cold.

I know that address.

Forget a demon autopsy. Willow wouldn't be joining him today because she would be dealing with the destruction of her office.

"Keep the body on ice until my return," he barked, turning around to head right back out again. As he sped through the streets, he listened to the voicemails summarizing the situation.

While he'd allowed himself to be distracted watching over the witch, the enemy had struck elsewhere. The disturbing thing was that it still involved Willow.

He didn't like it one bit.

While he didn't have a siren on his hood, Alistair still managed to have cars move out of the way, and lights change, sometimes abruptly, as he neared them. Little thrusts of magic ensured that he sped smoothly through the worst traffic knots, and sooner than expected, his truck roared to a stop a block over from the scene of the crime. Not that you'd know looking at it that anything had happened.

The dome of concealment showed nothing amiss. It also turned away anyone who had no business being there. It would only fool someone with absolutely no magic.

He strode through the barrier, like walking through a clear bubble with a slight popping sensation as he passed.

Inside, the calm mirage vanished. The stink of magic hung heavy in the air, layering the place. Some of it from the concealing dome, other parts the search-and-identify kind. There existed, as well, under the stink of ozone and fresh breezes—courtesy of the elves on staff—a hint of fire and brimstone. Demon.

More than one demon, he reckoned.

There were TDCM officers inside the cordoned area, collecting evidence in esoterically sealed bags. Also, one angry witch.

Alistair noted Willow, her hair dancing in a non-existent breeze, facing off against a young wizard, still wet behind the ears and using his badge as a pompous excuse to keep her out of her own building.

The kid wouldn't live long if he didn't learn to play nice with others. Was the body of wizards so lax in its training these days that it didn't teach them the basic respects, and the warning signs of a woman about to go off?

Willow's voice snapped, "Listen here, you little twerp. I don't care how much your daddy paid to get you a job with the TDCM. I am the high priestess and owner of this property. You can't prevent me from going in."

"This is a crime scene, ma—aaaaam." He squeaked the last bit as Willow lost patience and whipped out her hand, little stick clenched in her fist.

The wand itself didn't have magic; rather, it acted as a focus, and, in this case, directed her power to levitate the wizard, dangling him upside down.

Willow stalked past his screeched, "Put me down."

"If you insist." A flick of her wrist and the boy went crashing. He would have smashed his face against pavement had Alistair not provided a cushion of air. Willow would be in enough trouble having magic-handled the lad without adding personal injury to his claim.

Then again, the idiot shouldn't have stood in her way.

Alistair caught up to her just inside the warehouse, the people who would have stopped them both moving out of the way once they saw his upheld palm.

Wizards had no need for physical badges. They carried their authority around as a sigil on their hands.

He approached quietly to where Willow stood a few yards inside, staring.

The place appeared as if a tornado had

swept through the inside. Furniture, what little of it there was, smashed into irreparable pieces. Paper shredded and balled and plastered to walls. The stench of urine prevailed, the ammonia content high enough to make eyes water. Other fluids that didn't belong in her place of work scattered throughout.

"It can be fixed," he said.

"It stinks," was her retort.

"I'll have a team decontaminate and clean it for you."

"That's not necessary."

"Yes, it is." Because he said so.

"How did they know to come here?"

Leading her by the elbow, he guided her away from curious eyes to a corner empty of damage and people. "They probably came across the scent of many magic users in one spot."

"Or they found out our address."

"Demons don't hunt that way."

"I wouldn't be so sure of that." Her troubled green gaze met his. "What if they're smarter than we give them credit for?"

He trod carefully with his words. "The evidence thus far hasn't indicated they're more than beasts."

"Because we haven't wanted to attribute something intellectual to monsters. But what if we've been wrong? What if they are intelligent? What if there's a purpose to their attacks?"

No wonder Morfeus hated her. The woman was much too keen. She saw things. Things she shouldn't know. "Just because they lucked out and found your coven building doesn't mean anything."

"Then why did they steal all my coven files? And what of the writing you said they found by the Peabody crater? The one they brought you in to decipher? All along, we've been going under the assumption they're bloodthirsty animals. Hunting them as if they're simply predators with only one thought in mind. Survival. If they're more...then that changes everything."

He could have lied at this point and said demons were indeed dumb beasts who couldn't decipher her coven records. However, she wasn't stupid. Why steal them unless they could make use of the information inside?

"It's possible they're more organized and learned than the TDCM has admitted."

She pounced on his revelation. "So they can read the addresses."

He nodded, and she cursed.

When she would have stormed off, he held her, her arms slender under his grip, her petite frame bristling with anxiety, and fear. Trepidation not for herself, Alistair realized, but for the people affected by the theft.

"I'll have officers sent to the homes of your coven members to provide warning and protection."

"You don't have enough people to do that. You'll spread the TDCM too thin, and this isn't the time for that. I've already got Kal calling them and telling them to go into hiding." Willow sighed. "What a cluster. It's Salem all over again. Hunted because we wield magic. It's not something we asked for. We're born with it."

"And do you regret having magic?"

A startled gaze met his. "Never. I love what I do. I just hate that a matter of birth makes us targets."

"Then help me fight." Fight against those that would ruin this world like they ruined the one they tried to escape.

She snorted. "Fight how? We can't even detect them. Short of coming across one munching on someone, or walking on the ceiling, we have no idea who is possessed."

"So we need to find a method." One that didn't involve laying traps.

"Find a method, he says." She rolled her eyes. "You make it sound easy."

"Perhaps it is more simple than we know. We still have a body to dissect."

"You really think we'll find answers?"

From a corpse? Doubtful. "There's also that strange text we found. I've yet to show you."

Her eyes widened. "Do you think it has a clue that can help?"

Good question, and one he was unable to answer. Apparently, Morfeus hadn't been far from wrong when he'd declared the text gibberish. Despite all his linguistic learning, Alistair had been unable to decipher it, but he'd only just begun. "Only one way to find out. Will you join me?"

Her shoulders straightened. "Let's go. There's nothing I can do here."

Her resolve was most attractive, especially

with the hint of altruism laced through it.

His upbringing didn't see much of that. Most people he knew were about advancing themselves or their family. Male or female, it didn't matter in his world. Only power did. The concept of helping others was foreign and fascinating.

Stubbornness, on the other hand, was not.

"Get in my truck," he demanded for the second time on the sidewalk—because her tiny death trap offended him.

She shook her head, red strands flying. "I will follow you there."

"For a woman intent on saving the world, you are determined to waste gas."

"No, you are wasting gas." She pointed to his truck. "If anyone should be offering to carpool, it's me. Get in my car, or are you chicken to let a woman drive?"

"It's not your driving skills I'm calling into question. It's the ability of your car to carry me. Are you sure it can handle two passengers?"

"Cluck."

He glared. "It is not cowardice making me hesitate but rather a distinct lack of urge to compact myself into a tiny ball."

"You're not that fat."

"That fat?" He repeated the words a touch incredulously. "I am perfectly fit."

"If you say so. Now, are you getting in or not? I'll be coming back here after we're done, and I can drop you off. Or take your truck, and I'll meet you there." She smiled, the smirk taunting because she expected him to say no. To refuse to get into the tiny metal box and let her drive.

If there was one thing Alistair hated, it was predictability. He got into the passenger seat and tried to ignore how his knees touched the dash and his head skimmed the roof.

She gaped at him through her open driver-side door. "What are you doing?"

Fucking with her, obviously. He smiled. "Accepting your kind offer for a ride."

"But—"

"You're right. We'll save on gas. Just doing my part to save the world."

Literally.

Chapter Eleven

Having him sitting so close to me proved distracting, which might be why I sped to Fairy Fingers.

I'd been there before, once, before Morfeus hip-checked me out of the investigation. To those wondering, the Fingers location was a branch of the TDCM, the one dealing with bodies and organic samples. The TDCM had this thing about keeping its different departments separate. That, and the zombie uprising of 1908 due to an Egyptian artifact at headquarters had led to them to parceling off the morgue and labs. The seers also had their own place, on a mountain, high above any known flood lines. Sometimes, I wondered what exactly they knew.

To look at Fairy Fingers from the outside, you'd never know it hid one of the most sophisticated magical labs in the country.

First off, it wasn't in a glass-and-chrome monolith like so many pharmaceutical companies and businesses now gravitated toward.

The lab was housed in an older brownstone, smack-dab in the center of the city. Humans walked by the nondescript place every day, never realizing just how fake the advertised physiotherapist services were. Should someone who didn't belong enter, a very human-looking receptionist—a retired Valkyrie who could still wield a mean scowl when people tried to bully his or her way into getting an appointment—would turn them away.

Once past her, you entered a second reception area that required all visitors to sign in.

The receptionist, whom I knew—and hated because she didn't grant me favors like my friend did—never even glanced at me. Didn't acknowledge me at all as she gaped at Alistair.

Couldn't really blame her. The man looked delicious in a fresh pair of khakis and a V-neck shirt that hugged his upper body. He made it hard to remember that he was the enemy.

While Graciella usually kept her hair over her pointed ears, the flirty smile and head tilt meant that her silvery sheen of hair cascaded like a moonlit waterfall down her back, revealing the peaked tips.

I'd heard elven ears, especially the tops, were very sensitive erogenous zones. Which meant her showing them now was equivalent to a human wearing a short skirt and a low-cut shirt.

Hussy.

She batted lightly mascaraed lashes over brilliant green eyes that put my own dull ones to shame. Elven engineers had been the ones to create colored contact lenses, in part to combat the luminosity of their gazes. That simple invention turned out to be a monetary boon, as the vanity of people turned it into a billion-dollar industry.

"Please, state your business," Graciella purred in Alistair's direction, still not giving me the time of day.

It irked, especially since he soaked it up, proffering her a masculine grin that had me wondering how she'd look with short hair and no ears.

Jealous, and for what? A wizard. He and the elf were welcome to each other. I was here on business.

I stepped in front of him. "We're here for the autopsy of the demon brought in last night."

Finally, she spared me a moment. Graciella's lip curled. "Your viewing privileges were revoked when you were removed from the investigative group."

"I reinstated them," Alistair interjected, his voice low and sexy.

"And you are?"

"Grande Mago Fitzroy, here at the behest of the High Council of Mages. I belong to La Fratellanza Di Magia."

Graciella blinked. Blinked again, and the smile on her face was like the cat that ate not one, but a half-dozen canaries. "Such a pleasure to meet a man of your stature."

"Oh, give me a break." I rolled my eyes. "Can you save the flirting for when we're not dealing with murdering demons? We kind of have a time crunch thing happening here." Yeah, I was rude and bitchy and lying.

It bothered me that Graciella went after him so blatantly. It shouldn't. I mean, he wasn't mine by any stretch of the imagination, yet I really couldn't stand watching it happen.

Her brow tensed, and her lips pursed. It did nothing to detract from her beauty. Standing across from her—my clothes something I'd grabbed in a hurry, my hair a loose mess, and not even a dab of lip gloss—I felt distinctly disadvantaged.

I'd also probably grossly overstepped.

Alistair shifted to partially hide me. "My partner is correct. We are in a bit of a hurry. So if you could get us signed in and on our way, it would be much appreciated."

Look at him sounding so bloody nice. Still, it worked.

Graciella finally remembered her job. She slid forward a white container made of the woven branches of a rowan tree. "Remove your weapons and place them in the basket."

"I have nothing but my hands." He held them up.

As for me, I dumped my wand in and then my amulet. I already knew they wouldn't allow them to pass. Removing them, I felt rather naked. A witch never went anywhere without charms.

The basket disappeared behind the counter, and a perfectly manicured nail, long and squared at the end, the polish a shimmery pink, tapped the opaque surface. "Please sign in."

There was no pen or paper on the counter. But I knew what to expect. I placed my hand flat on the surface. It hummed and heated slightly with magic.

A bell chimed. Always a good sign. I'd

heard rumors of what happened if you weren't approved. Incinerated on the spot. Speared from the ceiling. I'd even heard claims of a pit underfoot.

None of that happened, although it did take a few seconds before the chime occurred for Alistair.

I shot him a side-eye. Graciella did, as well. But the chime gave him permission. She waved a hand to their left.

"You may proceed through the door."

Time for the next round.

I stepped through the frosted-paned portal, Alistair on my heels. The man crowded my space. Invaded my senses. He stood much too close in the small room we entered.

There was no furniture, the only decoration some silver hooks that marched horizontally across the wall. Two of them held white coats. Camouflage in case humans made it this far.

The magic in the room hummed, and a melodic voice ordered us to, "Assume the position."

Having done this before, I held out my arms to the sides. I held still with my eyes closed as the cleansing magic tingled over my skin, sterilizing me, including my clothes. No microbes or traces of magic would be allowed to pass to the inner sanctum.

The band of magic ran up and down my body.

At my back, Alistair chuckled.

"What's so funny?" I asked, keeping my lips

as still as possible. For some reason, I had an irrational fear of the magic getting inside my mouth.

"It tickles," he said.

The unexpected response had me peeking over my shoulder at him. He grinned at me. Standing much closer than necessary.

So near, I couldn't help awareness from flaring through me.

The hidden speaker snapped, the voice not as melodic, "Face forward and remain still."

The chastisement had me rolling my eyes. The spell to cleanse didn't really care about what position I stood in, but I obeyed, even as Alistair snorted behind me.

The light in the room grew brighter as we entered the last level of decontamination. My skin tingled, but not due to the magic sweeping over it. Alistair had stepped closer, close enough that I could feel the energy eking from his body. My skin heated.

His lips whispered beside my lobe. "If they were truly serious about checking us, they'd have us strip."

An innocuous statement, yet I couldn't help but imagine him taking off his shirt.

I clamped my eyes tight, wondering why he didn't get voice-smacked by Graciella for moving. Then again, he was a wizard high up in the food chain. Me, a mere witch.

The air in the room cooled, even if my skin didn't. The hidden speaker declared, "You are clear of enchantments and curses. You may proceed."

"And what would have happened had we been cursed?" Alistair mused aloud.

"Something painful, I'm sure." I'd had to preside over a few ceremonies to remove curses from coven members. It was never pretty and usually involved screaming.

What I did find interesting was that Alistair still looked as handsome as before. No glamour to make him better looking, and no spell of attraction.

It meant my reaction to him? One hundred percent pure lust.

Apparently, I had no standards when it came to good looks. Despite the fact that we weren't the least bit compatible, I craved him.

He can never know. While it was taboo for wizards and witches to get together, it did happen. It never ended well. Which went against some of my research into our origins because more than a few legends claimed that witches were the result of wizards mating with humans.

Yet I'd been taught that sex between our kind resulted in nothing. According to science, our genes weren't compatible. Odd given our resemblance physiologically.

But I wasn't here to mull over the mating capabilities of wizard and witch.

The door out of the sterilization chamber opened to a long corridor. A rather boring hall considering the magic that happened in this place. It consisted of a series of closed doors, identified with plaques. Again, and I knew this by rumor only, apparently opening one to which you weren't authorized would result in punishment.

The TDCM and its branches didn't mess around with possible spies.

There was a paranoia that went beyond the fear that humans might find out about wizards and their magic.

Personally, I thought the world would better receive the fact that we had Gandalf types among us than they did werewolves. But I could be wrong. Look at what my own kind did to witches back in the day.

Having been here before because of an autopsy on a witch, I strode down the hall to the last door, the one marked *Autopsy*. While the supernaturals didn't have high mortality rates, their healing abilities being advanced and disease almost unheard of, they did suffer accidents, and some non-accidental deaths.

Today, however, was about exploration. Alistair had brought in a demon corpse. I wondered what it would appear like. The very first demon problem had only smoldering chunks left when they were done killing it. The feline beast had grown strong before being taken down.

Peabody had never had a proper chance to feed, the host body having been captured and imprisoned.

This would be my first look at a true demon. Would it resemble those described in the Bibles and ancient texts?

If it did, then it would be proof they'd visited us before.

I didn't enter, raising my hand to knock. Only idiots disturbed the medical wizards working in this place.

Apparently, Alistair didn't harbor the same kind of worry. He grasped the knob on the door and swung it open.

A female snapped, "What do you think you're doing?"

Way to go. He'd managed to piss off the elder in charge. An elf I'd met during the last autopsy, who was a stickler for formalities.

Stepping around Alistair, I presented myself before the elven lady dressed in a scrub suit to protect her from splatter.

"Elder Kell'en, a pleasure to see you again."

I got a *hmph* in reply. I sensed more than saw Alistair stiffen.

"Have you gotten so old you've forgotten your manners?" he quietly inquired. Steel ran through his query, and the other woman's gaze narrowed.

"I don't know you."

"Odd, because I was going to say the same about you." Alistair sounded coolly amused.

"I am Elder Kell'en, second daughter of the Morning Sun," which made her related to the Elven king.

"And I am Grande Mago Fitzroy, sent here at the behest of La Fratellanza Di Magia, and the one who captured this demon."

"You did this?" The woman's eyes widened as she glanced from Alistair to the body on the table, covered in a sheet. "But how? It usually takes a team to bring one down."

"Probably because the quality of students

being accepted and their subsequent training leaves much to be desired. Where I come from, our entrance exams are much more rigorous, and our education more thorough. We don't tolerate weakness."

His words made me frown even as Kell'en's cheeks turned pink at the rebuke.

I thought all the wizard schools were the same. If you were an elf or some other acceptable race with magic, then you could go to school to learn. I'd never before heard of there being a threshold to enter. The coven certainly didn't apply any. Then again, most humans never even knew they had magic. It wasn't something they could easily wield with their mind and thought like the wizards could.

"I've brought my assistant with me to observe the autopsy."

"A witch?"

Having met Kell'en before, her snobbery didn't exactly surprise me. What did was Alistair's barked, "Where are your manners? Age is no excuse for forgetting them. This witch, as you so disparagingly label her, is the leader of her coven and deserves your respect."

Lips pressed tightly, Kell'en glared at me before spitting out, "Good day to you, High Priestess."

I blinked, mostly in shock. I don't think I'd ever heard an elf use my title before. Some of the other species did, especially at the ball where manners and polite dancing were everything. But, here, in a place where I didn't usually get so much as a head bob of acknowledgement?

Epic. I smiled. "May good fortune bless your house." The polite words had her gritting her teeth. I might have grinned wider.

Alistair clapped his hands. "Now that we've settled things, let us begin."

By begin he meant dealing with what lay on the table.

The autopsy room wasn't anything like those portrayed on television, although it did have some similarities. For one, it was pristine. Not a speck of dust or drop of blood anywhere in the white, sterile place.

The walls were unadorned. Only a single door marred one smooth surface.

No windows at all. A precaution in case the dead didn't stay dead.

For furniture, a counter rested against a pair of intersecting walls. They held stands filled with glass vials and beakers. There were a few propane Bunsen burners, another concession to modern day, mostly because it didn't leave a smoky residue on items.

Unlike a real morgue, there wasn't the astringent scent of cleaners or even the sweet rotting decay one expected. Elder Kell'en somehow managed to have the room smelling like a field of springtime flowers. Which made me twitch, given I was allergic to the real thing.

Only a suspended ball of magic illuminated the room. Nothing else was needed, given that source of light could increase its brightness on command as well as move around as needed.

Right now it hung right above the gurney, a change I'd heard from the previous practice of using stone altars. Practicality won out over old-school. It was much easier to wheel bodies around than have people carry them.

And that was it, unless you counted the stone grate under the gurney. Even magic couldn't prevent the spilling of blood, ooze, and other things. In the case of the dead rising, ashes could be sluiced into a containment area.

The first time I'd seen an autopsy done—not all that long ago I might add, the witch in question the first victim of the demon—I'd wondered at the lack of modern-day equipment. It seemed odd to not see any machines, not even a tray of tools. How would they slice into the body? How would they store specimens without a fridge?

I tended to forget the wizards' and elves' dependency on magic for everything.

Kell'en didn't do anything so mundane as pulling the sheet off the body. Rather, she fluttered her hand, and the covering lifted away, a ghostly shroud that compacted itself into a ball that ignited. The ash it created was contained in a force field, fascinating to watch. The bubble then pushed through the grate on the floor, disappearing from sight.

They didn't believe in washing stuff. Bleach couldn't get rid of everything.

Who cared about their laundry practices with a body in front of me? A rather human-looking body.

I grimaced. "He doesn't look very

demonish."

"I assure you, he is."

I paced around the gurney, remarking, "Where's the slimy skin, the horns, the hooves?"

Kell'en answered. "While his outward shell might appear human, he is not. Like the Lycans, he has the ability to morph his shape. The form he dies in is the visage he keeps."

"So how do we know what he looks like when shifted?"

"We don't," Kell'en replied. "Once they are dead, their true shape is lost to us."

"Not entirely true," Alistair remarked, breaking his silence. "It is possible to stimulate the body into performing one last shift. However, it requires any residual energy the body has left and only lasts a moment before turning it to sludge."

I wrinkled my nose. "Gross."

"How do you know this?" Kell'en asked sharply.

"We've been very thorough in our studies of the creatures."

"You've had some in Italy?" I hadn't heard the problem had spread beyond our continent.

"A few. This plague is not as contained as many think."

"The elven council will need to be apprised."

Alistair's lips twisted. "The elven council knows. They, and many others, have chosen not to release the information. They think it is but a passing issue of no import."

"No import?" I exclaimed. "The demons

are killing us."

"Killing human witches only thus far, hence their lack of foresight," he corrected.

"Idiots," I mumbled, earning myself a glare from Kell'en.

I resisted an urge to stick out my tongue at her. She—and others with her attitude—was the problem. They refused to listen. What would it take for them to realize the problem was bigger than any petty arguments?

I looked at the body and wondered what had made the demon choose it as a host. It certainly wasn't for looks. I doubted the pasty-skinned guy with thinning, greasy hair looked any better alive than dead. It wasn't for youth. He was pushing the hard edge of forty at least. Nor did he appear as if he lived cleanly. The yellow tips of a pair of fingers on his left hand indicated that he smoked. The broken capillaries in his nose pointed at a drinking problem.

"How does a demon choose a body?" I asked. "Or is it just proximity?"

"Proximity is the main factor. They need a host to survive in our world."

"But how do they jump from their world to ours if that's the case?" I asked. "If our world is toxic, then how do they hunt a body?"

"That part is still somewhat murky. It's been theorized that they can enter our world for a short period before expiring. In that time, they must find someone to act as host. Other researchers think that they attract suitable hosts to rifts, drawing them in and taking over the body before entering our world."

"Which might explain the situation at the Peabody house." If a rift had opened in the home, as the owner claimed, then it would be easy for the demons to claim the family. And the priest who'd supposedly gone to exorcise the home but got eaten by it instead.

"If you are done chitchatting, could we begin the autopsy?" Kell'en looked as if someone had shoved a lemon into her mouth it was so puckered. I wondered if it was the fact that she had to play nice with a witch or the obvious realization that the TDCM on this side of the big pond was so ill-informed.

Sharing wasn't caring in the supernatural world. While the TDCM was considered the ruling body in North America for wizards and magic, other entities existed elsewhere with La Fratellanza being the oldest known one.

I kept my bubbling questions to myself for the moment, but made a mental note to grill Alistair later. He seemed remarkably informed, and I would be stupid to not take advantage of the fact that he was willing to talk. I'd just make sure that, this time, he did the talking. No more hypnotizing me into spilling secrets.

The elder elf didn't use a scalpel to examine but simply hovered her hands over the body. My teeth vibrated at the magic she oozed. I couldn't see what she did, but she at least intoned her findings—with her eyes rolled back in her head, which gave her a freaky look. So long as she didn't start hovering and cackling, I figured I was safe.

"The organs show signs of change at a molecular level. There is also growth, alien in nature." Her hands paused over the heart. "This has doubled in size and is encased in bone. A denser bone than the rest of the body."

"Meant to prevent direct blows from killing it," Alistair muttered.

The hands began moving again. "A secondary organ, similar to the heart, had begun forming here." The groin area. "And there is a strange growth on the stomach."

"Where they store the magic," Alistair explained. "It's what you need to stimulate to get the body to change."

"The brain appears unchanged, however…" Kell'en's brow drew together. "There are more neural pathways than normal for a human."

"More pathways than even an elf," Alistair corrected.

Which fed into my growing belief that the demons weren't dumb.

It seemed a little freaky to see the mouth on the corpse suddenly open wide. Just the elder doing her thing, but I shivered anyhow.

"Elongated canines."

The better to eat witches with.

"Eyesight receptors changed."

"To improve their nighttime vision. They can also see magic once they reach a certain level of change."

Alistair kept spouting facts, and each time, Kell'en stiffened.

The rest of her monologue for the front of

the corpse proved of no interest. I might have looked away when she spent some time over his penis. A single penis, I might add, with no teeth, unlike legends that claimed a pair for demons.

"Turning the subject over." Magic levitated the body and flipped it face down. I immediately noticed the lumps by the shoulders.

"What's that?"

The elder sounded surprised when she said, "The beginnings of wings."

Which meant the lump above his butt? Yeah, he was getting ready to pop out a tail.

Just what would he look like fully changed?

"You said, as they get stronger"—aka better fed—"they can change into their natural shape. Yet..." I pointed to the protuberances. "The first demon we know of looked like a giant cat. So it had a tail and giant teeth, but no wings."

Alistair replied. "The reason is twofold. Firstly, they do retain some of their host's attributes. And secondly, much like we have a varied population on Earth, so do the demons come in different varieties."

"How many?" I asked.

"How many do we have here?" was his retort.

The idea that there could be dozens, or hundreds, of different types of demons proved chilling. If one giant kitty demon could almost take out a group of wizards, then what if we faced a handful? An army? A—

"If you're done inspecting, Elder, would you like to see what this particular specimen looks like when he's not wearing a human host?"

No. "Yes."

It amused me to see that I wasn't the only one stepping away from the table as Alistair drew close to it. Elder Kell'en also took a few paces back, but neither of us looked away as Alistair held his hands over the abdomen.

He explained as his hands shimmered, the intense magic from them making them blur. "It takes power to change, unlike the Lycans, who do it naturally. Each time they change, they must feed to replenish before they can change back. The longer they are here, the less they need magic as their demon self merges with the human host, adapting to the Earth's environment."

As he spoke, I noticed the body on the table shiver then rise, hovering mid-air. The skin on it darkened, the pale flesh giving way to something darker and slick. Hairless, as well. Sickening crunches as bone reformed, and the limbs changed shape. The skin expanded on its back before bursting open, the wings hinted at by the nubs exposed. The tail unfurled to be long and barbed at the tip. The fingers were clawed, and each hand had a sixth digit.

It proved morbidly fascinating to watch, and sickening, as well. This was one of the creatures hunting the coven.

Most of them, barely past the first level of training, would never be able to prevail against a monster.

They don't stand a chance.

The body was still changing when Alistair

barked, "Contain it."

Kell'en didn't hesitate. Her hands rose and cast a bubble around the body, and just in time.

It exploded into black goo, a thick slime that coated the magic bubble and made my stomach roil.

I didn't even want to imagine the smell. Even less the reminder that it used to be human.

And now it was sludge.

Not much was said after that. Kell'en looked like a lemon tree had crawled up her ass and stalked off. Whereas Alistair didn't appear disturbed in the slightest. Then again, this wasn't his first demon autopsy.

I feared it also wouldn't be our last.

We left the morgue and got back into my car. It surprised me to see that he respected my cone of silence. The knowledge he'd imparted turned round and round in my head.

How did he know so much? Some of it could be attributed to his examination of prior bodies. But other things stuck out, such as his ability to bring one down single-handedly. His knowledge that they partially bore the shape of their host. That a multitude of species of demons existed.

And then there was the fact that the TDCM knew nothing at all. International boundaries shouldn't apply to matters of grave import.

Then again, the Fratellanza had finally sent over their demon expert. Surely that counted for something. Perhaps a cooperative effort was finally underway to combat this seemingly growing problem.

Blame my riotous thoughts for me not noticing the SUV that came barreling out of nowhere. In my defense, it shouldn't have happened. My light shone green. Traffic was halted, yet that didn't stop the large vehicle from careening into the opposing lane's traffic and driving through the intersection. Right at me!

I was a Smart car stuck in headlights.

I screamed like a girl and braced for impact.

Chapter Twelve

The lights caught them as a vehicle ran the light, attempting to ram. Willow noticed.

The impressive screech—at decibels that almost shattered glass—hadn't even finished emerging from her body when Alistair had his hand aimed out the window.

Witches used wands and familiars to focus magic. Wizards used their bodies.

Alistair focused his will and his power into his hand and projected it as a flattening shield to protect the car. It had no real shape or substance—anyone looking wouldn't see a thing—but they sure as hell saw the result.

The SUV hit the opaque shield, full speed, and crumpled in on itself. They had but a moment to gape at the screaming, twisted metal and hear the screech of tires as people braked all around before they shot past the wreckage.

Shot might have been pushing it. Her tiny car put-putted along, motor straining at the fact that it had to propel two humans instead of mice.

Still, they emerged unscathed, but not safe. The SUV accident was anything but accidental.

"If I were you, I'd go faster," he urged, turning to look over his shoulder as more vehicles, with a lack of regard for lights and rules of the road, piled in after them.

Two by his count, plus one that had just careened out of a side street ahead of them and whipped sideways to box them in.

"Why?"

"Because we're under attack."

"I am being attacked!" she squeaked. "What the hell? What do they want with me?"

"You are assuming it's you they want."

Willow shot him a brief glance. "Are you really going to argue that it's all about you at a time like this?"

"It wouldn't be an argument if you admitted I am the most likely target."

"Most likely to get throat punched for being an arrogant ass," she muttered as she suddenly turned the car into an alley in an attempt to evade their ambushers.

"There is more afoot than you realize," he admitted.

"What a surprise, the TDCM and all the wizard outposts in the world are hiding shit." Her sarcasm dripped heavily.

"There are some things that mortals aren't ready to know."

"In case it slipped your notice, we're all mortal, just some more than others."

By that, she meant that while humans now enjoyed a longer lifespan than their ancestors, they still couldn't come close to that of elves or many other creatures. Alistair didn't deign to use the term supernatural. There was nothing super about them. Every species had its quirks. It just turned out that humans were less tolerant of differences. Since they reproduced quickly, and in rabbit-like numbers, it forced those different from them into hiding.

"Your little maneuver didn't work. They're still following," he observed, rather than enter a lively discussion about how humans couldn't handle the truth. He'd save it for later.

"I'm not blind," she grumbled, shooting out the end of the alley, narrowly missing a woman pushing a stroller. She also managed to squeeze in between two moving cars. His Hummer would have never made it.

Then again, his Hummer wouldn't have had to run out of fear of getting squished like a bug.

"We need to get to TDCM headquarters. They won't dare attack there," he said.

"Too far. I doubt we'll make it. I know a place that's closer."

She didn't elucidate further; instead, she hunched over her wheel, weaving in and out of traffic, even into the bike lanes as she sought to give them some space. However, her tiny car remained limited in what it could do. It lacked the daunting size and aggressive ability of the other vehicles that charged ahead and forced traffic out of their way.

They shot out of the city, the sudden green space a surprising choice. Out in the open, it would be harder to hide. Yet she appeared to have a plan, or at least knew where she was going because she careened around a few corners before slamming to a stop in front of a cemetery.

"This is your safe place?" he asked, unable to hide his incredulity.

Willow didn't reply as she scrambled out of the car, the open door letting in a familiar smell.

Green grass, freshly turned earth, and oh, the putrid stench of ghouls.

This wouldn't be good.

Chapter Thirteen

I didn't know who chased us. However, I was pretty darned sure we'd need some help. Sure, Alistair appeared pretty handy with the magic, but he was only one guy. One fellow against a tiny army? Even he would run out of power. The well of magic we could draw from wasn't never-ending.

With four cars chasing us, and who knew how many people—or things—inside, we needed help, and fast.

Most supernatural folk would have put a call in to the TDCM. They might have even answered, given who was with me in the car. However, they could be notoriously slow, especially if they didn't consider the incident worthy of their attention.

I had no proof of who attacked. It could be humans. A case of mistaken identity. Carjackers.

Okay, maybe not carjackers, but without proof of a supernatural attack, the TDCM wouldn't lift a finger.

Good thing I had other friends. Friends who wouldn't bury me in red tape and reports afterwards. A friend who owed me for setting up a deal with the local morgues to help feed his children.

That friend was why I screeched to a stop in front of the cemetery. I hopped out and noticed Alistair not moving. "Let's go." I peeked over my shoulder to see that we hadn't lost our tail. The pursuing vehicles were coming in fast.

"No need to worry. I can handle this." He stepped out of the car, nonchalant as you please, and turned to face the approaching SUVs.

He didn't do anything fancy. Didn't roll up his sleeves—then again, he didn't have any. Didn't strike a pose or make some grand declaration. Alistair simply stood between me and the barreling vehicles.

Nutjob. I wasn't about to become road kill; thus I headed into the cemetery.

A loud crack made me peek over my shoulder.

The front windshield of the lead vehicle had exploded outward, and a giant fireball came blasting toward us.

Even from this far away, I could feel the heat. The kind that melted the flesh off bones.

Alistair had a bored expression on his face as he held up his hands and generated the same shield as before. This time, since I wasn't concentrating on surviving, I could see its indistinct, wavering shape. A flat panel to deflect.

The fireball hit it and didn't disperse. It kept pushing, the flames of it licking sideways, looking to feed on its target, and failing. I might have felt more optimistic if that initial blast hadn't been joined by more fireballs.

Two, three. Alistair wasn't breaking a sweat.

Still, he had to be feeling the strain.

As for me, I was panicking a bit. This was hardcore magic. Deadly. I had to do something to help. I could have whipped out my wand and added my strength to his, but I hadn't come here for nothing.

I bolted into the cemetery proper, yelling, "Beetlejuice. Beetlejuice. Beetlejuice." There was no real magic in those words, just a running joke I had with the person who lived here. An ancient vampire who no longer wanted to deal with the world but had to because of his ghouls. I'd befriended him by accident—his ghoul had tried to eat me, and I'd brought him back to his owner and given him hell. That was how I met Marcus. He admired the fact that I'd not outright killed his child. I couldn't, not when the ghoul reminded me of one of my favorite movies with its crazy hair, pasty skin, and striped pajamas.

It became a joke between Marcus and me that it would be my code phrase if I ever needed help.

I fucking needed help.

Luckily, Marcus wasn't asleep, and unlike legend, sunlight didn't do shit to his skin. However, he wasn't happy about me disturbing his gardening—which no one ever questioned. Apparently, folks who felt a need to pull weeds in cemeteries were best left alone.

He leaned back on his heels, a youngish looking man, his dark hair held back in a ponytail, his straw hat floppy, the brim protecting him from the worst of the sun's rays. His well-worn jeans had dirt on the knees, and his shirt hadn't seen better days in at least a decade.

To those just meeting Marcus, he looked like a hippy, a babe barely able to shave until you looked into his eyes.

Stare too long, and you started to babble. I'd heard some people even pissed themselves because, in his gaze, they saw nothing.

It was scarier than it sounded.

"What have you done now?" he asked, peeling off his gloves.

"Under attack," I said, huffing. Running should be left to those who thought marathons were fun.

Marcus turned to look at Alistair, still holding his shield, barely discernible for the flames licking at it. "From whom?" he asked.

"Who do you think? The guys lobbing fireballs."

"Interesting," Marcus mused aloud. "And what do you think I should do? I am not a fire hydrant to put out fires."

"We have to do something."

Marcus sighed. "You do realize if I unleash them, I probably won't be able to stop them."

I nodded. "I know. But this is kind of an emergency." Especially since I didn't know who attacked us and why. Fireballs seemed to indicate wizards, but who would be stupid enough to attack us?

Or was Alistair right? Were they only after him?

If that were the case, why was it that the

things pouring out of the SUVs' backseats were headed toward the cemetery and not the grand ol' wizard?

"What are those?" I asked, not recognizing the loping creatures on all fours. They had tails that pointed skyward, and they uttered god-awful screeches.

"Imps. What did you do to get on their radar?" Marcus muttered. "And who was stupid enough to unleash them in the city?" Standing, Marcus stretched to his full height and tilted his head back. If the situation weren't so dire, I might have admired his shape a bit more. The man was gorgeous—but terrifying. Especially when he whispered, "Rise, my children." The words brushed past me, cool, dark, and shiver-inducing. "Rise. It's dinnertime."

By children, he didn't mean baby vampires like him. Nope. He was talking to his ghouls. His progeny.

There were many stories and legends about ghouls, a mishmash of facts and fiction.

Fact: vampires made them. They were the ones the vampire curse—or blessing as some chose to view it—didn't work on. Not everyone could become a bloodsucking minion. Those that failed to transition became ghouls, almost mindless creatures who lived for flesh and blood, often mistaken for zombies because they didn't take care of themselves. But ghouls didn't rot like the undead did. They did, however, hide in graveyards among the dead. Burrowing underground, feasting on the inhabitants. Only when they ran out of stuff to eat did they become a problem, which was where I came in.

I'd helped Marcus create an arrangement with certain groups in the cities. Hospitals that needed to dispose of organs without evidence—and cheaply. Morgues. The supernaturals also found Marcus and his children useful for disposing of bodies that might cause questions.

Rarely did his children get to eat something fresh, though.

Today was their lucky day.

At first, I didn't see them. They were just shadows peeking out from behind gravestones. But those shadows moved, slinking across the ground on all fours, their dull and dirty clothes a dark blot across the green grass. While they all started life the same way, once turned, it wasn't long before all traces of humanity disappeared.

Preferring the dark to the light, the ghouls grew pale, so very, very pale. Their hair almost always turned white, as well, as if the very idea of pigment was leeched from their bodies. Their skin hung on their frames, all their fat siphoned by the burning need for flesh. As for their eyes…black holes that showed no compassion, nothing but hunger.

The ghouls loped across the carefully tended grass—Marcus kept the garden for his children clean. Even from where I stood, I could see the drool hanging from their slack lips.

Most of the charging herd, a dozen or so, went after those emerging from the trucks—and oddly enough, heading for me. However, a few veered off toward Alistair. Not surprising. They weren't the brightest creatures.

What did shock me was Alistair doing something to his shield, some kind of bend in it that directed the flames onto the ghouls.

"No!" I shouted as the fire hit their bodies. He was killing our allies. Not exactly a good idea with their maker standing beside me.

I went to move to stop him, but Marcus placed a hand on my arm. "Stay here."

"But he's killing them."

"He only does what he must."

"But they're your children." Of sorts.

"They are mindless animals, who live tormented by the fragments of who they used to be."

"If that's the case, then why haven't you killed them yourself?"

"Because I cannot do what must be done. I made them but lack the courage to end them."

"And you're okay with this?" I swept a hand at the unfolding carnage.

"They are abominations. They should be destroyed." He sounded so nonchalant, yet I wondered how much of his stoic expression hid the turmoil and anguish inside.

Surely, it bothered him?

Stunned, I could only watch, riveted by the unfolding fight, which resulted in short-lived screams.

The imps didn't die quietly, and neither did the men in the SUVs who emerged with automatic rifles.

The *rat-a-tat-tat* tore into ghoul flesh but didn't stop the attack. Of the dozen or so that started the dash, a half-dozen remained, and they swarmed the living in a carpet of moving limbs and gnashing teeth.

All too soon, the enemy was gone, the fireballs extinguished.

The fight was over. But the ghouls didn't understand that.

They turned toward Alistair, and I took a step forward, murmuring, "No." It didn't stop what happened next. The remaining ghouls loped toward the wizard, and I gripped Marcus's arm. "Tell them to stop."

"I can't." The resignation in his tone bothered me.

"Stop!" I shouted. "You don't have to kill them. We'll call them off." I took a step forward as Alistair ignored my words.

The fireballs were gone, and I couldn't tell from this distance if he still held the shield. His hand was raised. A moment later, he began to lob his own fireballs. Not bright orange ones but mauve, a color I'd never seen, but effective. The short bursts of heat ignited the ghouls one by one and burned them to ash.

Until there were none.

No one left but me and the vampire, so was it any wonder I shivered when Alistair turned toward us? Even from here, I could see his expression. A blank mask of nothingness.

A chill went through me that had nothing to do with the breeze outside or the cloud that covered the sun's rays. It almost appeared as if Alistair's eyes had turned black. Surely a trick of shadows because, as soon as he walked toward me, I saw the bright blue I'd come to know.

The fierce scowl, however, was new. He ignored me and focused on Marcus.

Before I could make introductions—and duck out of the way in case Marcus took revenge for his children—Alistair boomed, "How far has your kind fallen that you would knowingly allow so many travesties to live?"

I expected Marcus to blast him. To, at the very least, tell him to fuck off. To my eternal shock, he dropped his head. "Blame the weakness of an old man who wanted children of his blood yet didn't have the strength to make true ones or get rid of the ones that failed."

He apologized? For some reason, it bothered me, especially since Alistair maintained his thunderous expression.

"Stop harassing Marcus," I snapped, jumping in. "His ghouls saved us."

"I had the situation in hand," was Alistair's terse reply.

"Only until your shield failed. And then what?"

The dark grin he tossed my way sent a shiver through me. A sensual one this time. "I would have killed them all."

Despite the bold claim, I believed him. There was something about Alistair that was different from the other wizards. An assuredness for one, but he also appeared much more powerful than anyone I'd met before.

So very, very strong.

A man who could keep up with a resilient witch.

What the hell am I thinking? Wizards and witches didn't mix.

"Who were those people?" I asked Alistair. "And why would they be coming after you?" And me.

"I have many enemies."

"Understatement," coughed Marcus.

"There are those who don't want me to help the TDCM."

"Who sent them? Those were imps." Things of legend, supposedly from another dimension, and capable of surviving on our plane but hard to control. It was why wizards had banned their use.

So who called them?

"A rogue faction, I imagine," Alistair replied, but I didn't trust his answer. I sensed he knew more.

"Were they after you or me?" Or both of us? Was someone working with the demons? Was this their attempt to stop our investigation?

"Me, of course."

I rolled my eyes. "In case you didn't notice, your pompousness, they were also coming after me."

"Why would they do that?"

"For one, I'm a witch, and wizards, even one working against the TDCM, are predisposed to hate me. Speaking of wizards who hate me, I'm pretty sure Morfeus would like it if I disappeared." The man had a hate hard-on for me, and now that he'd been demoted, I wondered if he blamed me. However, would he have the balls to send an attack force after me?

"That man had better not be behind it, or he'll find himself dusting the wind," Alistair snapped. He turned his attention to Marcus. "No more ghouls. I mean it."

"Yes, my lord."

"And don't call me fucking lord." Alistair turned on his heel and stalked to my remarkably undamaged car.

I took a moment to lean up on tiptoe to brush Marcus's cheek and murmur, "Sorry," before following.

His reply. "Be careful. He's dangerous."

No shit. The man had taken on not only an attacking group armed with fireballs and guns but also ghouls, and he wasn't even sweaty.

How unfair. I, on the other hand, had perspired in my run across the graveyard and could feel my hair curling in damp wisps around my temples.

Alistair veered from my car toward the empty vehicles. The doors remained wide open, the ground around them grimy with blood and body parts.

Usually, we wouldn't see a single drop. The ghouls tended to devour their victims right down to the last knucklebone. Had they not turned en masse on Alistair, they would have licked the ground clean.

While my wizard did a circuit around them, upon reaching the first SUV, I poked my head inside and gagged. "Smells like something farted in here." Farted, sweated, and a bunch of other gross things.

Lovely.

Still, I needed information before the cleanup crew got their hands on this crime scene. I'd fired off a quick text to Kal as I left Marcus.

I wasn't worried about the humans noticing. Marcus kept a spell of look-away on his cemetery. How else could his former children frolic among the graves?

A peek into the glove box found the registration papers. One Dick Harrelson. I kind of had a feeling Dick wasn't the one who'd been driving.

Chances were these vehicles were stolen. But stolen by whom? I'd not recognized anyone in them. At least the ones I'd seen. Wanna bet they weren't registered wizards with the TDCM? Did they come from another country, or was this really a rogue group? It was, after all, possible, given the covens certainly hadn't gathered all the potential witches out there. We kind of had to rely on either stumbling across those with the talent or hope they sought us out.

A peek in each of the vehicles didn't reveal anything except the fact that imps stank. No secret map to some evil headquarters. No name of the guy who'd sent them.

Just another dead end.

And more mystery, I added as I turned around

and saw that Marcus had followed us and knelt on the ground in front of Alistair.

Alistair placed his hand on the vampire's forehead, but I couldn't hear if he said anything. I do know Marcus shot him the most beatific smile.

That of a supplicant meeting his god.

Exactly who was Alistair Fitzroy?

It was past time I found out, and only one person I knew was qualified to dig out the secrets I wanted.

I took my time getting to my car, giving the guys time to finish whatever weird ritual they were doing.

When it was done, Marcus headed back to his graveyard, and a more relaxed Alistair returned to me.

As soon as he got close, I said, "I don't know about you, but after a day of break-ins, dissection, and now ambush, I could use a good meal. Care to join me?"

It didn't take his brows shooting skyward for me to realize I'd surprised him. Despite it, he managed a hasty, "I would be delighted."

Let's see how long he remained *delighted* once he met my mother.

Chapter Fourteen

They didn't stay for the cleanup. Alistair pulled a few strings when he reported the incident. Usually, he and Willow should have stayed behind to place a report. However, there were advantages to rank.

He called in a cleanup crew from the TDCM and cited confidential High Magi business. That stopped further inquiry.

For now. Eventually, someone would demand answers, but by then, he hoped to have some. Such as who the faction was that had so openly attacked.

After everything that had happened, Willow remained surprisingly quiet during the car ride to the restaurant. Very unexpected. Given her inquisitive nature, Alistair had anticipated her lobbing questions at him. He'd even prepared how best to dodge them, especially the explanation of Marcus's deference toward him.

That one could prove tricky. Vampires usually deferred to no one outside their kind. So what would he tell her? The truth? Or the same lies he told everyone else?

You can't tell her the truth. No one was ready for that. Not now, perhaps not ever.

The close confines of her car proved

distracting, the scent of her wrapping around him, a mixture of fading adrenaline, smoke, and her. The essence of a woman.

Quite intoxicating. Everything about Willow drew Alistair, and the more time they spent together, the worse his attraction got. Alistair should have been focused on his mission and that alone. However, who said he couldn't mix a bit of pleasure in there? Perhaps by satisfying his carnal need, he'd find himself more clearheaded.

Count on a male to find justification for sex. But would it just be sex? Usually, his body didn't crave so loudly. Usually, he could turn off his desires at will.

All that had changed when he met Willow.

The silence continued but for the soft crooning of a song on the radio. Alistair wondered what ran through her mind, especially given her surprise invitation to dinner. And where exactly would they eat? They didn't have the kind of attire or freshness to dine anywhere public, at least not anywhere with decent repast.

I don't want greasy fast food. Perish the very thought. Yet he'd swallow the overly processed excuse for sustenance if he had to. He wanted to spend more time with Willow—and not just because she was crucial to his case.

She intrigues me as a woman. A desirable female who is fearless and quick-thinking. Someone who shows a will of iron yet has an inner softness. Just look at her reaction when he destroyed the ghouls. Most rational beings would eliminate them on sight. However, she'd worried about her friend.

A witch, friends with a vampire, and not because she served as a blood slave. She was the most surprising creature.

Such an ill-timed distraction… Yet, he didn't mind so much because, in her, he could see a glimmer of possibility. An option he didn't yet dare contemplate.

"Exactly how strong are you?" The question, breaking the silence, proved startling. Especially since it wasn't one he'd expected.

"I don't work out at a gym if that's what you're asking."

She let out a sound of annoyance. "Don't play stupid. I mean magically. How strong are you?"

"Strong enough to be a Grande Mago."

"Still not an answer. You are powerful enough to hold up a shield for quite a bit of time against several attacking wizards. A large barrier, I might add. Manipulate it. And then throw off mauve fireballs, a color I didn't even know was possible, and still look like you could have handled more."

"I could have." It stroked his pride to realize she'd noticed.

"Most wizards can't do that. Not without taking a break in between."

"I'm not most wizards." Not even close.

"What are you?"

Much like at their first meeting, she asked, recognizing his difference. "I'm a man." Physically, at least.

"But not an elf."

"Nope."

"This is where you say, 'hey, Willow, I'm a…'"

"What do you think I am?"

She slapped her steering wheel. "Would I be asking if I knew? It's driving me nuts because here's the thing. You don't look anything but human."

"Humans can't be wizards," he replied by rote.

"I know, which is why I wish you'd stop beating around the bush and tell me. What are you?"

The conversation might have continued if her phone hadn't rung.

"Answer that, would you?" she growled.

"Do I look like your secretary?"

Her fiery temper emerged, and she snapped, "Would you like me to answer it and possibly run us into a tree?"

"Testy, testy," he teased, enjoying the fire in her. He fished her phone from the console. She didn't have a passcode, he noted, so it took only a swipe of the screen to answer.

"Hello, you've reached Willow's phone. How may I help you?"

"Um, who is this?"

"Alistair Fitzroy playing secretary to the coven priestess."

She snorted.

"Well, this is her other secretary, calling to say I'm going to head home for the night."

Alistair repeated the words to Willow as he

put the phone on speaker so they could both hear.

"How many on the list did you manage to contact?" she asked.

"Not enough." The tinny reply caused her shoulders to droop. "I left messages where I could. I'll call a few more when I get home. I didn't want to be out after dark."

"You shouldn't be going home at all. I want you to hit a hotel. The coven will cover the bill."

"I'll be fine," Kal retorted. "It's still daylight, and my boyfriend is coming over tonight. Once he's inside, I'll be sure to spell all my doors and windows."

"Not exactly reassuring since I know your lawyer friend is like totally anti-violence."

"Kenny? We broke up a few weeks ago. I'm talking about Martin, the marine. And he's got great big guns." Kal snickered, and the jest drew a faint smile from Willow.

"Let me know when you get home safely."

"Will do, boss."

"Did you happen to see Whiskers at all today?" she asked.

Kal replied. "No. But a neighbor popped by to complain that she saw an orange kitty in her yard chasing the birds. Claimed there were feathers everywhere."

"Well, at least he's not going hungry. And if that was Whiskers, then that means a demon didn't steal my kitty after all."

"Do you want me back at your place in the morning, or should we attempt the office?"

She shot Alistair a look.

He replied, "I think it best if you take some time off for the next little while. Perhaps go somewhere and not tell anyone, not even Willow."

"Do you think they'll target Kal?"

His jaw tightened. "Everyone with magic is a target. If you value his life, then I highly recommend a vacation until we get the demon situation under control."

"I guess I'm taking my vacation early then, boss."

"Be careful," she said. "Text me to let me know you're okay."

"Will do."

The phone went dead as Kal hung up, and Willow was silent, but only for a short moment.

"Do you really think we can get the demon thing under control? We don't even know how they're getting here."

"Soft spots."

"Soft spots from where?" she growled. "I'm getting tired of you being stingy with your information."

"My information is considered classified."

"By whom? The wizards? What a surprise they don't want anyone to know. Your tight lips are costing lives."

Lives he usually had no connection to. It caused his brows to draw tight. "I will divulge some of what I know, but keep in mind, what I'm about to tell you is hypothetical, and secret. The soft spots that are allowing the demons to pass into our world are a planetary rotation thing. An alignment of universes if you will. Once the two worlds move out of alignment, the problem will disappear."

"So these soft spots acting as doors will close. Will the demons leave then, too?"

"Not the ones already in our world. But when that time comes, we will hunt down those remaining."

"We just need to hold on, then. How long before our worlds shift away from each other?"

Good question. He'd yet to figure out the math behind it. "No idea. But this isn't the first time this has happened."

"I figured as much. At least I know we survived it once before. And with less technology. Which should make things easier, I guess."

Survived, yes, but not in the way she thought. He kept that part to himself.

When Willow pulled to the curb of a house, a two-story, cookie-cutter home on the outskirts of the city where suburbia started, he stared at the area. Then stared at her, noting her amused smile.

"Where are we? I thought we were going for dinner."

"We are. But I wasn't in the mood to change and shower, so I thought we'd come here."

"And where is here?"

The door flung open, and a woman with the same red fiery hair—an older version of Willow—emerged with arms extended and a bright smile. "Willy! Why didn't you tell me you were coming?"

Willy?

The witch emerged from her car. "I wanted to surprise you. Hope that's okay. I brought someone with me."

Alistair emerged from the car and prepared to introduce himself, only to find himself in need of possible medical attention given the ear-piercing scream, "You brought a man!"

In that moment, a cold fear invaded him, one he'd not felt in a long time.

No. She didn't. Oh, but she had. Willow had brought him to meet her matchmaking mama—he recognized the gleam in her eye.

And judging by Willow's smirk, she'd not brought him because she wanted him as a mate. She was up to something.

His gaze narrowed.

Challenge accepted.

Chapter Fifteen

Taking him to my parents' place was a risk. For one, we'd just been attacked. What if I led some bad guys there?

My brothers would probably thank me. Given that usually one or more of the six of them came for dinner every night, chances were good I'd have backup if we were attacked again.

Not that I truly needed extra help. Alistair seemed more than capable of handling danger. It made the man super sexy. But still off-limits.

Mother, however, wouldn't care about that. I could already see the gears in her head working.

I'd brought a man to the house. I never did that, mostly because I wanted them to call me again and not run the other way when they saw me next. My family could be a bit much.

So why had I brought Alistair? It wasn't as if I considered him serious boyfriend material. *He'd make an awesome lover, I'll bet, though.*

Yet he could never be anything more because I didn't think I could trust him.

There was something sly about him. Mysterious. Since subtle prying wasn't my forte—I preferred bluntness and was often compared to a bull in a china shop—I'd let my mother wheedle secrets out of him. He would probably fight it, but by dessert—something hand-crafted and decadent—he'd collapse like a house of cards.

No one could resist my mama's cooking.

Entering my childhood home, you'd never know the place used to be a chaotic nightmare of running shoes, jackets, and book bags strewn all over. The scuffed wood floors used to bear the marks of boys running through the house, sometimes in their cleats. The walls always appeared dingy with handprints and scrapes.

That had all changed the day Mama shoved her last baby bird from the nest. And I mean shoved.

Once college was done, she had us out applying for jobs every day, and as soon as we got our first paycheck, she evicted us. Then demanded we return for dinner at least once a week, more being preferable.

The house transformed after we left. Now when you walked in, there was white marble tile—spotless, without a speck of mud—and a closet, with hangers for coats. The sideboard table held a basket, and the rule was, if you wanted food, drop the phone in it.

I pulled mine from my pocket and tossed it in. When Alistair didn't copy, I leaned in and muttered, "There is a no-phone rule during dinner."

"Really?" His brows arched; however, he smiled as he yanked his cell out and tossed it with nonchalance into the basket with the others. "How refreshing to go back to simpler times where entertainment came from actual interaction."

Mother must have heard. She didn't reply, but I noted the way her head tilted.

A scheming tilt, I should add.

The main floor no longer had walls separating the spaces. Dad had torn those out. The ceiling was now vaulted, exposed thick beams running across, and in between the stained wood, white drywall, bearing recessed pot lighting. Very modern and chic just like the white stone fireplace with its gas insert.

Gas, not wood. My parents had become so civilized with age.

Would the same thing happen to me?

Bypassing the immaculate couch set, not covered by a sheet to hide the holes and stains, we hit the open-space kitchen. Mother had no upper cabinets along the back wall, just a window running from the countertop to the ceiling overlooking the oasis they'd made of the yard.

The almost one-acre property, deeper than it was wide, no longer boasted a dirt track with humps for stunts. I'd bet the neighbors breathed a sigh of relief when we moved out. We weren't exactly quiet children growing up.

"Can I offer you a drink?" Mother asked, giddy with excitement but remembering her manners. "Beer, cocktail, iced tea. Freshly made, of course."

"Iced tea, please."

I didn't bother putting in my order; Mother knew what I liked. Perhaps she could explain why I kind of liked Alistair.

There he sat on a stool, looking relaxed and at ease. In my kitchen. With my mother. Alistair had yet to bolt or devise an excuse to leave. I was a little surprised. Most wizards wouldn't have deigned to cross our threshold. Associate with mere humans? Perish the thought. Yet, here he was, a man high in the order, politely conversing with my mom.

Why? This wouldn't advance our demon case. Surely, he had other places to be. Things to attend to.

Then again, so did I. *I should be finding out what happened to the warehouse.* As well as helping Kal with the task of contacting my coven members to ensure that they got to safety. I hoped they heeded the warning, especially since night was about to fall.

With the dark came the true danger.

"So you're working with Willow?" Mother finally deviated from topics like the weather and the flowers in her garden to tackle the real stuff.

Perching on a stool, I leaned in to nibble off the platter of appetizers she'd set out.

Yes, appetizers. A great big tray of them. Yet, so far, despite the blue car in the driveway, I'd yet to see a brother, or even my dad for that matter.

As I crunched into a mini quiche, Alistair verbally danced with my mother.

"Yes, ma'am." Ooooh, look at him being all polite.

"Please, call me Ann."

"And you must call me Alistair. Your

daughter has graciously agreed to help me with a case."

More like bullied.

"She's a smart girl. Reckless sometimes." My mother…praising, yet at the same time, humbling—in a single breath.

"Sometimes chances have to be taken to get the job done."

Nice one.

"Are you from around here?"

A subtle poke.

"No. I'm actually from Europe."

"Your English is impeccable."

No sign of an accent. Did he speak more than one tongue? Say like French?

He casually leaned an arm on the counter. His lips tugged into a partial smile. "I went to a very good school."

"Majoring in?" Mother probed.

Alistair played tight with his answers, but Mother could be more tenacious than a terrier, yet so cute while doing it.

About the same height as me but more rounded. "*Seven kids will do that to a woman,*" she liked to exclaim. But my daddy loved her curves, so it was never an issue.

Mom always wore a smile, now at least. When we were kids, she swung between grins and scowls. To be fair, we usually earned those scowls. As mentioned, we weren't exactly a quiet bunch. Nor were we bad. We did have a lot of energy to expend, though, and not all of it constructive.

"Should I perhaps forward you my

resume?" A naughty glint entered his eyes, not a magical one, but one borne of mischief.

Uh-oh, was he seriously going to mess with my mom?

This would be good. I grabbed a handful of kettle chips and slid the ramekin of dip closer.

"I don't think a resume is necessary. You can summarize the main points, I'm sure." Mother didn't back down.

He laughed. "Forgive me for being lax." He gestured with a hand. "I am Alistair Fitzroy. Thirty-seven years of age—"

A little bit older than me.

"I was born in Brisbane, England. But only lived there for the first year. Then I resided in Italy for the next thirteen years of my life. I've been to France, Germany, and even did a stint in Australia."

"And now you are here, in the USA, doing important things." I threw that out there and earned a twitch of the nose from my mother.

Don't interrupt the process.

"What are your qualifications?" Mama interrogated.

"My linguistics skills," he said with a pointed look at Mama, "came about as part of my studies at Oxford."

"Oxford? But—" I bit my tongue before asking why he hadn't attended a school for wizards. Mother didn't know he was a wizard, and as far as the world was concerned, they were only something seen in movies and dungeons and dragons games.

"But what?" he said, his lips curved in a mocking smile. "Oxford is an excellent school."

"For humans." Mother saved me. She didn't look at Alistair as she wiped imaginary crumbs from the counter. "You're not human."

"What am I then?" he asked, not at all perturbed by my mother's assessment.

"Your aura is interesting, I don't think I've ever seen the like." Mom glanced at him, her eyes slightly out of focus. "But if I had to guess, I'd say wizard."

He shot me a glance. "I didn't know your mother was a witch."

"Not a witch." Her lips twitched. "But I do know things."

And now that his secret was out in the open, I could ask the question bubbling at my lips. "If you went to Oxford, how did you learn magic?" Because his studying at a human school made no sense. My understanding was, to be considered a wizard, with all the rights and power it entailed, you had to study at an approved facility.

"I have what you might call a natural aptitude for wielding magic. I also had a very educated wizard father who ensured that I was properly trained from a young age. It allowed me to skip the usual methods."

"And the Magi Council accepted that?" I couldn't help a skeptical note.

Again, he flashed white teeth. "Oh, they didn't receive me easily. I had to go in front of the High Council of Magi and submit myself to a rigorous battery of magical tests. I passed them all.

When I proved that I was as good as and, in many ways, *better* than their graduates, they had no choice." His smile widened, and, yes, it was cocky, but he wore it well.

"A powerful wizard, in my house. Goodness," Mother exclaimed, fanning herself. It was beautifully done. An outsider would sense the mockery, yet not be able to pinpoint it.

Alistair didn't miss a beat. "I hear your daughter is a strong witch. Did she inherit from you?"

Mama tittered. "Me, birth a witch? I think she got most of her handy potion skills from her father."

I had. But...

That was when Papa entered. A dapper man in his sixties now, he had grown out his hair and his beard. He also wore pressed khakis and collared shirts.

My dad, the yuppie version of Gandalf.

"What did I do?" he boomed. A big man, my daddy towered over most people.

Not Alistair. He stood and met my dad, hand outstretched.

"Alistair Fitzroy. A pleasure to meet you, sir."

"He's working with Willow. On a case." The subtle intonation my mother gave the words made me roll my eyes. Way to divulge that I sometimes spilled about my work to family.

Then again, they had a right to know what might murder me. Daddy didn't like things that could kill his little girl.

"What kind of progress are you making on the demon incursions?" Where mother subtly pulled, Daddy smashed.

It was a neat combination. Guess who I took after?

Alistair's gaze narrowed. "We're working on a solution."

"While you're all dithering around, witches, like my Willow, are being targeted."

"The TDCM is doing what it can."

"In other words, diddly-squat." Daddy didn't mince words. "Bunch of textbook boobs, they lack an imaginative brain among them. But I guess they can't help that seeing as being a wizard handicaps them."

Alistair's mouth snapped shut.

My daddy brushed past us to drop a noisy kiss on Mother's cheek. He might look like a yuppie version of a fantasy wizard, but inside, he was a boisterous soul.

I heard the front door open and a voice.

"Where's Willy? I saw her car out front."

Pivoting on my stool, I tossed my brother Rowan a wave. "Hey. Come on over and say hi to a bona fide Grande Mago." No point in hiding Alistair's status anymore. He was about to realize that my family was a little more learned than most.

"Him, a Grande Mago?" Rowan snorted, his big shoulders shaking. "As if. He's too young to be a pompous ass."

"Language," mother barked.

A grin lit Rowan's face. "Sorry, Ma."

He would be if he swore again and she

heard him. Mother wasn't too old to tackle his ass and wash his mouth out with soap. It helped that the boys didn't move or twitch when she did it. Daddy would have killed them if they acted against my mom.

"You must be Willow's brother." Alistair introduced himself. While Alistair wasn't quite as big as my dad, he did match Rowan for size.

"So how's the demon hunt thing coming along?"

I might have winced as my brother dove right in.

"He probably can't talk about it. Who knows what would happen if the masses found out about the demons. Why, they might get guns and other weapons to defend themselves." My mother wielded her sarcasm as she whipped a roast out of the oven while flipping in some buns and solving world peace.

Okay, she didn't do the last bit, but she could if you gave her a big enough kitchen and a megaphone.

If Alistair was shocked by my family's verbal attacks, he didn't show it. "There is no reason to panic. There have only been a few incidences."

"If by few, you mean seventeen," Oak declared, entering the kitchen from the hall.

"Seventeen?" Alistair's brow creased. "I think you're mistaken."

I snared a few carrots to crunch on as I moved to the table set with a full ten-place setting. The table could have handled more. Mama liked entertaining.

"Your office probably doesn't know about thirteen of them. Not everyone enjoys sharing with the TDCM."

Just like a wizard, he fell back on the rules they were so fond of. "The treaties between the groups state full cooperation on matters that cross boundaries."

By boundaries, he referred to the species one. If something happened that could affect another group, they were bound by law to tell the others.

However, each group kind of made their own decisions on what to tell or not. "Cooperation between the species has always been an issue."

"What makes you think your incidences are related to the demon matter? Seventeen is a rather high number considering we've only registered four confirmed cases."

"Because you're not looking." Yeah, I couldn't help the jab. I was having fun watching the usually calm and collected Alistair scramble.

"Speculation says we'll be at nineteen cases by tomorrow," my brothers Banyan and Ash declared. The twins walked in, just in time to sit down as the platters of meat hit the table.

Thick slices of roast beef, all the kinds you could like from well-cooked crust, to barely pink, very pink, and still cherry red.

I liked mine pink, and I speared a piece before handing the fork to Alistair.

As we ladled food, introductions were made. Again.

At times, I wondered if it wouldn't be easier to just wait and do it once after everyone filtered in.

When the eating began, Alistair was the one asking questions. "What's the evidence you have linking the cases?"

Impressive. He appeared to sincerely want information rather than pulling a pompous dick move and insisting they spill and desist from all other actions. The TDCM honestly thought they were the only ones qualified to deal with magical issues.

Personally, I sometimes felt they were the most unqualified to do so.

Once again, Alistair appeared different from all the other wizards I knew. For one, he didn't call me something derogatory. No hearth witch nickname or the *more* derogatory broom bitch. If they were really trying to be funny—and asking for a throat punch—they liked to ask if my pussy needed a rub.

Let them laugh and mock all they wanted. I knew the truth. They were no better than me.

In between inhaling food, Banyan replied, "If you mean evidence like folks getting torn apart, then, yeah, we've got some."

"It's not just the demons," Alistair argued. "Lycans, trolls, actually a whole host of other creatures could be responsible."

"Except they're not just mauling and eating them; they're sucking out the magic." Oak raised his gaze to Alistair's. "That's demonic activity."

"And it's not just witches being eaten,

which has been all the TDCM has covered thus far," Rowan stated before devouring a tiny loaf of bread.

"We've gotten word of a flight of fairies getting gutted. A mermaid. Two non-practicing elves. And more."

If Alistair looked doubtful before, that had changed. He now bore a most serious mien. "Are the locations of the incidences you're mentioning relatively close to one another?"

Banyan shook his head. "They're happening across the country, and those are just the ones we're one hundred percent positive about."

It appeared my brothers had been industrious. Just not busy sharing the info.

I drummed my nails on the table. "And why is it that I'm just now hearing of this? What happened to reporting to me when you got the goods?"

"We would have if you ever showed up for dinner," Rowan retorted.

"I've been busy." Working. Still managing to call my mother but avoiding the gatherings. Mostly because I was tired of showing alone.

Never mind that my brothers usually didn't bring their girlfriends around, I could almost see the disappointment in my mother's eye that her only daughter wasn't settling down. She wanted to give me a princess wedding. I'd never admit it aloud, but I kind of wanted it, too.

Would Alistair make a good husband? It couldn't happen, not with a wizard, but I did wonder.

Would he be an attentive partner or a distant one? A day ago, I might have had an answer, now...I had to wonder.

I glanced at Alistair as he conversed with my six brothers, Sylvan and Linden having arrived and jumped right in. Late as usual, and together. We rarely saw the twins apart.

Alistair turned his head and caught me staring at him. I felt an unusual heat rise to my cheeks and turned away, only to discover Mom watching me.

Oh, shit.

I tried to engage after that, grilling my brothers for more info—where, how, and why the murders had happened. Apparently, they'd all just returned from their trips, and they promised me reports.

The gist? Various places with no rhyme or pattern, the victims ripped apart and eaten, their magic gone.

The news was both good and bad. It meant that witches weren't the only things on the demons' menu. With more of the supernatural population impacted, it was more likely we'd see forces marshaled to combat the problem.

The bad news was, there was more than just one demon, which meant multiple soft spots between our worlds. So many doorways for them to spill through.

This could be the start of a war.

Speaking of wars...I fought my own skirmish after dinner.

Round one: dodge the mommy who wants

grandkids.

"So, he seems nice," Mother said when it was just the pair of us in the kitchen, the boys having gone outside.

"We're work partners, nothing else." Not yet.

Not ever! Why did I keep having to remind myself?

"Why did you bring him?"

"We were hungry."

"Plenty of restaurants around."

"But none have food as good as yours." Yeah, I buttered her up.

Mom saw right through it and snorted. "You wanted me to check him out."

I shrugged as I dried a plate and put it away. "Maybe. He's hiding something."

"Aren't we all?"

"I don't know if I can trust him."

"Why does it matter if you're not planning to date him?"

"Because I want to know he has my back in a fight."

"Judging by your clothes and stench, I'd say you already know he does."

My mother could be too damned perceptive at times. "He's not what he seems."

"And that bothers you because you like him."

"No." We both heard the lie. "It doesn't matter if I do. You know the rules. Wizards and witches don't mix."

"You know what I think of rules." Mother

drained the sink and then turned to lean against the counter, ignoring the men outside tossing a football. Never mind that we had a demon situation. They were out in the yard, almost daring one to come. Knowing my brothers, they were really hoping a demon would be stupid enough.

"It's not just the rules, Mom. I have responsibilities. I need to take care of the coven."

"Being a leader doesn't mean you get to ignore your needs. I've seen how you look at him. You're attracted to him."

"A little."

"If you are, then there's no harm in indulging."

"Are you seriously telling me to have a one-night stand?"

"I'm saying to stop being so damned responsible and perhaps do something for yourself for once. Have sex with Alistair. It might do you some good."

Not too shocking in and of itself. It was realizing that Alistair had entered the kitchen and heard my mother that had me fleeing.

"Gotta pee." I ran past him, cheeks hot. But even hotter? The blood coursing through my veins.

Could I be so selfish and do something just for pleasure?

Why not?

Chapter Sixteen

Willow took off as if imps nipped at her heels, leaving Alistair with her mother.

"She's a good girl. Smart. Pretty. Stubborn."

"You don't need to sell her to me," Alistair replied. He already knew all those things. Plus the fact that she had a close-knit family. Very close. So tight, her daddy had whipped the football at him while casually announcing, "Hurt my daughter, I hurt you."

Then the brothers, one by one, with wide smiles, also threatened him. In direct contrast to the mother, who thought they should sleep together.

He preferred the latter suggestion.

They took their leave, Willow emerging from the bowels of the house, refusing to meet his gaze and saying they should go.

She suffered, with rolled eyes, the bone-crunching hugs of her siblings and father, almost hit the floor with the bag of leftovers her mother bestowed upon her, then led the way out of the house.

A *home*, he corrected, full of love, and a surprisingly well-informed family.

Had the TDCM cut themselves off so much

from the world that they truly were the last to know?

The car ride proved quiet as she whipped through the streets. Tension hung in the air, sexual tension, he'd wager, given her flushed cheeks.

"You have quite an interesting family," he noted, not willing to remain quiet.

"I do."

"Are your brothers and father witches like you?"

"Not quite. They have some magic, but they're not into the whole potion and coven thing."

"Do you have any more hidden siblings, or was that the lot of them?"

"That's it for my immediate family. We won't talk about my extended one."

"Why? Family rift?" He knew all about those.

"You could say. Mom's family disowned her for marrying my father. Daddy, on the other hand, was an only child."

Which might explain the large family he'd created.

"I don't have much of a family. Only my father is left." The tidbit he revealed was surprising, given he rarely mentioned anyone related to him.

"That's sad."

"I guess. We aren't close." Understatement. Hard to maintain a relationship when those related to you wanted to kill you to move up in position.

"Yet you still followed in your dad's

footsteps. Your father is well known as an expert in things ancient and magical."

"My knowledge was from curiosity, not the urge to emulate another."

"I can understand that. I was always poking my nose into everything as a kid. I read all the time; whereas my brothers preferred action."

"Who do they work for?" he asked.

"I can't say."

The reply surprised him. "What do you mean, you can't say? Aren't they employed by the coven?"

"Nope. If they were, they would have been reporting to me directly. I'm just lucky they like me enough to share."

"Then who do they work for?"

"My answer of like fifteen seconds ago is still the same. I can't say. But I will throw you a bone. The TDCM isn't the only agency out there."

Something more secretive than the wizards?

Now that shocked him.

They pulled into the warehouse district, and he noticed her tensing beside him. Night had fallen, a thick blanket of darkness and shadows where anything could hide, and from which predators liked to hunt.

"They won't attack," he said aloud.

"They? So you do think there's more than one?"

"According to the mess found within your building, I believe we're looking for at least three."

"A hat trick of demons, and you're telling me not to panic?" She snorted. "That's like telling a gazelle to ignore a pride of hungry lions."

"If she doesn't bolt, then they won't always attack."

"If she doesn't, she's also baring her neck and saying 'eat me.'"

He smiled at her words. "I would be delighted."

"What? No," she stammered. Quite flustered.

"Shame. Let me know if you change your mind." A brazen speech from him. What happened to not getting involved with the witch?

I spent time with her.

He planned to spend even more. She had secrets. Alistair wasn't a man to leave a secret alone.

Willow halted her car by her warehouse but didn't stop her engine or get out. The unmarked TDCM vehicles from before had left. The containment field hiding their activity from passersby had dissipated, leaving just a forlorn building with only his truck out front.

Missing its tires.

"Son of a bitch!" he exclaimed, jumping out of the vehicle to run to it.

Upon first glance, he assumed human thugs. They would see his big new tires as a prize they could sell for a few hundred bucks easy.

But as he neared his truck, he sensed it. A tingle along his exposed skin. A subtle shift in the air.

We are not alone.

He'd no sooner thought it when the bloody

witch exited her car and said, "Shame about your wheels. I'll give you a ride to your place if you want, and you can call to have it towed."

"Get in your car." He barked the order as the air around him tightened, the tension in it almost palpable.

The very molecules wavered, and they stepped from the nothingness as they dropped the cloaks camouflaging their presence.

Five of them. A perfect squad.

Someone was getting desperate to eliminate him. First, the brazen daylight attack using peons. Now, a second one that might prove tricky.

He'd have to be fast. Sneaky. And not distracted.

Which meant Willow needed to move away. Yet the fool witch neared him. "Are you deaf? Those are demons."

"I see that."

What she didn't see, apparently, was how dangerous they were.

"Hide behind me."

A full-throated laugh met his request. "Not a chance."

While he tried to get Willow to do the right thing, the demons got closer.

And closer.

They didn't speak

They'd better not. It might be hard to explain how they knew him.

The demon with the burnt blue skin and tufts of dark brown fur—remnants of the animal he'd commandeered—stood on his hind legs.

Intelligence shone from its eyes. Its mouth opened wide in a toothy grin. It was going to talk.

Alistair raised his hand and fired a magical missile of light. It speared the demon through the head, and it fell, uttering an oomph of surprise.

Of course, his preemptive act had the others rushing to take him down—but not talking. He could handle that. He fired another bullet-like missile, only to have the demon deflect it. The surprise move wouldn't fool them again. At his first sally, they'd woven shields.

Even better, unlike the afternoon's attack, this time, he faced more worthy adversaries. About time they showed him some respect.

Alistair pulled on the magic, making it become an extension of his arms, glowing blades that projected from the knuckles on either hand. They weren't real knives in any sense, but they could deal devastating damage once he got past the shields. He'd have to hammer at them first.

He dove at the closest demon, shoving his weight into the attack, sending the male reeling. When the demon's back hit the ground, he landed atop him and began to pummel the shield, feeling the magic bend under his blows.

He pounced off the demon body just as another slashed down with claws extended. The scrape of real claws against magic rivaled nails on chalkboard.

Screeee.

He spun and lashed out, trying to trip his attacker. Only to get tackled from behind.

There was no such thing as a fair fight with

demons. He fought, finally breaking a sweat, unable to just lob magic like he could with most other species. Demons wielded magic like others breathed air. It was a part of them.

The only true way to kill them was by surprise, like he'd done to the first opponent, or through a battle of strength and skill, slugging and slashing, looking for a killing blow. But four against one weren't great odds, he had to admit, as he got slammed to his knees.

He immediately staggered back up.

A vibration underfoot caused him to wobble.

What's happening?

He ducked the slice of some claws and turned his head to see Willow behind him, holding a pair of demons at bay.

Actually, she held them in concrete, as in sunk to their waist, unable to extricate themselves.

She had her wand pointed at them.

"Finish them," he shouted then grunted as a fist caught him in the ribs.

"I want to talk to them first," she stated, tucking her wand under her arm and heading toward them.

Talk? No. No talking. Alistair could do nothing to stop her as a demon took him to the ground, its large, moist body landing atop his. Sliming him with its acidic saliva. It burned.

He heaved the other demon off, and then before it could recover, he stalked toward it, hammering it with short bursts of magic. The white light smashed against its body shield, pummeling it until it shattered.

The demon opened his mouth and said, "The legion—"

Flick. The ball of mauve fire engulfed him before he could finish his sentence.

The other one Alistair had been fighting tried to run.

Alistair threw out a lasso of magic and reeled him back in, looping the magical rope around and around and then pulling it taut. Squeezed tightly, the demon poofed. Gone from this plane, its host nothing but a pile of dust.

Alistair turned on Willow to see her in front of the demons.

And dammit, they were talking.

Chapter Seventeen

"Why are you here?" This was the second time I'd asked. The first time the reply was a wad of phlegm that I handily deflected and sent back in his face.

The wad of goo might have been hotter by then, as in boiling. The demon noticed and complained.

"Hello, talking to you." I snapped my fingers, but the demon with the now half-melted face didn't reply with anything coherent amidst his whimpers.

"Pussy." I might have sent a magical flick at his ruined flesh. He cried out.

Some might have questioned my somewhat violent methods. Those people hadn't seen a witch torn apart by one of these demons. They would have gladly done worse to me if given a chance.

"What about you, ugly?" I turned to talk to the other demon I'd sunk into concrete. A good trick to know when working against bigger numbers.

"Come closer, and I will tell you everything you wish." The other demon, his skin holding a sickly yellow hue mixed with green, licked his flat lips. He had a more human appearance than his friend, but given the somewhat reptilian texture to his skin, I suspected both of them had animal hosts.

The key word being had. These demons were obviously more evolved than the others I'd seen. For one, they had the wings projecting from their backs. Not big enough to fly, but definitely more than just useless nubs.

How much more killing and magic would they need to fully become? It made my blood run cold to think that these mental parasites exerted enough power to not only take over a host body but also essentially change its physical makeup.

I approached the chattier one but kept out of reach of those claws. Mom hadn't raised a complete idiot.

"Who are you?"

"Your worst nightmare."

I rolled my eyes. "Is there like a handbook all evil demons get? You know, the one that gives you cliché answers. Because, seems to me, you all have a hive brain. Don't you think for yourselves?" Or did we have a Borg situation on hand? If you didn't know what that meant, then time to brush up on your *Star Trek*.

"We are one in our purpose. One in our task."

"You are one because you suck," I noted. I inclined my head. "Looks like it's down to just you and me."

"You are no match for me," it hissed.

"Says the demon stuck in pavement. So, tell me," I whispered, leaning closer, teasing it. "Are all of you this easy to beat?"

Mother liked to use subtle nudges. Father was direct. As for me, I was the taunting one. The one who mocked.

Unlike some people, I enjoyed villain speeches. They tended to reveal a lot.

"We are legion. The army that never ends."

"Your legion sucks. Take a look around, visually challenged one. You and your buddy are the only two left, and if you ask me, your buddy's a bit of a wuss."

Spit-demon had stopped whimpering and glared. I waggled my fingers to say hello and mouthed, *Don't worry. You're next.*

He snarled and strained to reach me. "In a minute, ugly. I'm dealing with your friend." I jabbed my wand in his direction and gave him something new to whine about.

"Foolish witch. Bow down now and agree to serve your new master."

"Bow to you?" I snickered. "Not happening."

"Then you will die with the rest. Your world is ours for the taking. We are but the vanguard."

"From where? Do you have your visas up to date? Government isn't too keen on border-hoppers overstaying their welcome these days."

"You can't stop us. There are doorways opening everywhere. Bodies for the taking. Magic for the eating. Once we find a few of the true bloods, we won't need to borrow inferior bodies at all. Soon."

"Borrow? Does that mean you have a body

somewhere else?" The very concept boggled the mind. I mean, where did they leave it? What if their body died? What about when they died here? What happened?"

I wanted to know.

"Yummy witch. Come closer, and you will understand. Or will you ask the lord you work with?"

"Who?"

"The lord who betrayed the branch. He who is hunted—"

Zap. The laser of light entered between the demon's skull between its eyes and left a perfectly round hole the size of a quarter. Nothing came out of that hole. The edges of it singed dry.

The light of life, and evil fervency, faded from the eyes a moment before they shaded into gray then chunky dust.

Before I could tell Alistair to stop trying to help, he'd killed the other demon, too.

I whirled on him and planted my hands on my hips. "Did you have to do that?"

"Demons are dangerous."

"Well, duh. But could you not see I had them under control?"

"What I saw, *witch*," finally an inflection from Alistair, "was you using magic you shouldn't. That wasn't human witch magic."

"I have no idea what you're talking about. I used my wand, and look, even tossed a few herbs for my spell." I pointed to the ground at the scattered green and brown bits.

He looked at it and snorted. "We both

know that is just a pile of savory crap. You've figured it out, haven't you?"

"Whatever do you mean?"

"Now who's playing stupid?"

The jig was up. I cocked my head and smiled. "Why don't you tell me what you mean?"

"I mean the fact that some witches are, in fact, wizards."

My smile widened. "I prefer the term sorceress."

Chapter Eighteen

Alistair did not appear all that shocked by my announcement, yet he should have reacted.

Most wizards would probably expire of a heart attack on the spot at the idea a human, yes, a mere human, wielding their precious magic. Strongly in some cases.

I would know. I was a sorceress, on par with any damned wizard I'd wager, not that I'd ever actually been tested. What use did I have for snotty ritual and magic schools? Unbeknownst to the snooty Magi, the covens catered to all kinds of magical levels, from the novice and barely more than an herb witch, to hardcore, spell-casting, magic-weaving sorceresses or, in the cases of boys, sorcerers. We eschewed the wizard title.

We were more than that, and proud of it.

Just not proud enough to flaunt it. The last time we'd gotten cocky, the Inquisition happened. We learned after that.

I gave Alistair a side-eye. "You aren't surprised."

"Because I knew your kind existed. I've always known. But the fact that you're one of a special few and can sling magic doesn't mean we should stick around here waiting for more demons."

"You think there might be more?"

"I'd almost guarantee it."

"Care to explain how you know?" *And while you're at it, explain who and what you are.* Because, as more and more puzzle pieces fell into place, I didn't like the picture it formed.

"I have access to certain information."

"Because of your connections at TDCM?" I prodded.

"Of sorts." A skirt to avoid an outright lie.

"You know, I am getting mighty tired of your bullshit."

"Says the woman who's been pretending to be a simple witch."

"Never claimed I was simple, and you assumed I was nothing more."

"Because you don't exude the right kind of aura."

I snorted. "Neither do you. I guess we're both good at hiding what we are from the world."

"How did you learn to use your power, and don't tell me the coven. We both know they're mostly comprised of humans with weak traces of magic."

"I was home-schooled."

"Home…You mean your father is a wizard?"

"No. He's a witch."

"Your mother…" His jaw dropped.

"And you never suspected, Mr. Look-at-me-I'm-so-big-and-powerful-in-the-magic-world." I snickered. "My mother is a sorceress, as was my grandmother and her mother before her. It runs in the female line of our family."

"And the agency doesn't suspect?"

I blew a raspberry. "The agency couldn't find its ass with two hands if its pants were dropped. They've got it set in their minds that humans aren't good for anything but potions and charms."

"What of your brothers? Are they home-schooled sorcerers, as well?"

"Yup," I said. "But they're nowhere near as strong as I am. Do we have to do this right now? In case you hadn't noticed, we're kind of standing over a few grotesque bodies. I don't suppose there's any point in bringing them in for autopsy?"

"No."

I waved my hand, dropping the pretense of a wand. The corpses ignited, not the pretty purple flame he'd managed, but a respectable orange one.

He added his magic to mine, the purple wisps dancing among the copper until the demons' bodies were nothing but ash inside two giant potholes.

I'd have to call the city and get them to fix it.

Since there was nothing left to do here, I headed back to my car—a vehicle that he might have mocked, but look whose wheels were still turning.

"Where do you want me to drop you?" I asked as Alistair joined me and we set off down the road.

"Wherever you're going."

"I am going home."

"Sounds good."

At that, I slammed on the brakes and stared at him. "Excuse me? I am not taking you home."

"Oh, yes you are."

"Is this because of what you overheard with my mother?" I hissed. "Because, I assure you, that was her suggestion, not mine."

"Your mother is astute. She wouldn't have said something if she didn't think there was a basis."

"My mother is desperate for me to settle down with a man. Any man," I added, lest he think he was special.

"So, you're not seeing anyone?"

"My personal life is none of your business."

"It might be if you have a friend who will take offense to me joining you in your home."

"You are not coming home with me." I slapped the steering wheel for emphasis.

"That's where you're wrong. From this moment on, you and I will become close companions. We've been attacked twice in one day. Add in the fact that your warehouse was hit, plus the footprints in your yard..." He shook his head. "You are not spending the night alone."

"Gonna sleep in my bed, too, to make sure nothing can get me?" I snapped.

"If you insist." Said so deadpan, yet when I peeked over at him, I caught him staring, his expression quite smoldering.

At me.

I focused on the road. "I can take care of

myself."

"I noticed. Which is why I think we should partner. You're much more practical as a partner than any of those idiots the TDCM tried to pair me with."

"You want us to be partners?" Surely, I'd misunderstood.

"I'm just as surprised as you. However, this attack has shown that things are snowballing. It would be foolish of me to spurn your aid. You not only have the magic to defend yourself, your information sources are also obviously much more effective than mine."

"So you're just using me for my spy network?" For some reason, that made me feel both better and worse. Go figure.

After that, I ignored Alistair as best as I could and focused on the road. The fact that I'd handled two demons didn't mean I wanted to do it again.

There was something primitive and alien about them, but familiar, too. They frightened me. Especially now that I'd seen how they could fight.

I'd noticed Alistair moving lightning fast, wielding magic as a weapon against monsters that weren't even phased by it. Their use of a magical shield as body armor was something I'd never even heard of. I made a mental note to tell my mother. If they could do it, then, with practice, I'd wager so could we. But we'd better learn fast.

With the magic encasing their bodies, and the speed at which they moved, it hadn't taken me long to ascertain that I wouldn't do well in a head-to-head battle. Hence the melting of the pavement below their feet.

Surprise captured them. I couldn't count on it working every time, though.

The demons were dangerous opponents, and as the hour grew late, the pockets of shadow ominous, I couldn't help but realize that this was their playtime. In the day, I might hunt for clues about them, but at night, they stalked people with magic like me.

The fact that five of them banded together to attack only proved my earlier theory. These weren't mindless beasts. They invaded with a purpose and cunning. It concerned me, yet, oddly, I found the presence of the man beside me more concerning.

Why did he insist on protecting me? That wasn't how things worked. Even though he knew I was a sorceress, his human equivalent, he was predisposed to hate me. To ignore me. To not give a damn about my plight or that of my coven.

Yet he'd stuck close to me all day long. Why? What was he after?

And why did he know so much about the demons? Was he working with them?

He killed some tonight.

To maintain his cover, or because he was truly on my side?

Pulling into my driveway, I turned to stare at him. "What do you want?"

"I don't suppose you have hot cocoa."

The reply took me aback, which was why I didn't stop him when he grabbed the keys from my hand and hopped out of my car, heading for the front door.

Leaving me behind.

So much for his previous gentlemanly actions where he asked me to stand behind him for protection. Now that he knew I was a sorceress, he went dashing off to the house.

Only my dwelling wouldn't let him in.

The moment the key—a key he held—entered the lock, the runes went into play and grabbed him. They also cloaked him from view. Neighbors tended to freak when wannabe robbers were stuck to doors and crying for help.

I stepped up to him and smirked. "Usually, guests wait to be invited in."

"I was going to ensure your place was clear."

"Looked more like you were hoping I'd cover your ass." A fine ass, but still.

"There's nothing outside to worry about."

"And nothing inside to worry about either. Or did you really think I'd leave my home unprotected?"

"Nice spell on the door."

"Thanks." I had to wonder if he could bust out of it. Probably, although I'd prefer he didn't. This one had taken hours to craft properly and tether. I placed my hand over his. *"Tous sommes bienvenues,"* I said in heavily accented French. Not all of us had an education abroad. After this was all over, perhaps I could finally find the time to visit.

As soon as the door opened and I entered, I headed to the back. I wanted to check for myself if

Whiskers had returned. The food bowl on the deck outside remained untouched.

If it hadn't been for Kal's message from the neighbor today, I might have lost hope, especially since the messages I'd posted at the nearby humane shelter and on the lost pet network hadn't yielded anything yet.

I'd give it a few more days, but I couldn't wait forever. A pet was needed to maintain my cover. A witch had to have a familiar to ground her for certain spells. Cats were preferred, even if owls were capable of handling bigger magical loads. But they were also much messier.

Truth be told, I enjoyed having something warm, furry, and purring snuggling with me at night.

For some reason, I eyed Alistair as he prowled past, checking all the rooms. I doubted he'd purr, but I bet he could roar.

Bad witch.

Heading away from the door into the kitchen proper, I pulled out a mug from the cupboard and a little plastic K-cup.

Mother would have put on a kettle and boiled the milk fresh, then measured out real cocoa and sugar for the drink, adding marshmallows and a hint of cinnamon.

I threw the instant hot cocoa mix into the machine and, a moment later, slapped the mug on the table.

Alistair took a seat as I leaned against the counter, arms crossed. "I think it's time you started talking."

"About?"

"You."

"I thought your mother had already grilled me on my childhood, and your brothers on my occupation."

"Basics, and not what I'm talking about. Who are you?"

"Alistair Fitzroy."

"Like hell." I held up my phone. "I had some digging done." By Kal first, and then my brothers. As dinner had occurred, they were checking him out—claiming bathroom breaks but really heading down to the basement to run database searches. I waggled the screen at him. "Says here, Fitzroy didn't have any children."

"Not legitimate ones."

"You're not his bastard."

"No, we're not related." He stood, ignoring his hot cocoa, and my kitchen felt ten times smaller.

I swiped my phone and showed him another memo. "Says here, you didn't graduate from Oxford or any other school. Or, if you did, it wasn't as Alistair Fitzroy."

"Sometimes, a man needs to wear many names in his lifetime."

"Are you a man?" I asked, and he stepped closer, so close I could have reached out and touched him. So near, the scent of him surrounded me and I almost closed my eyes in the enjoyment of it.

I didn't know what the scent was. It was both exotic and foreign. Something I'd never encountered, despite all the playing with herbs and ingredients in my life.

I kept my gaze on his face—his intense expression, his blazing eyes.

"Who are you?" I breathed the words, and they didn't stop him from stooping. From bringing his mouth close to mine.

From brushing my lips.

Sigh.

I exhaled in trembling pleasure. I should have pushed him away, yet didn't. Hadn't I been waiting for this kiss from the moment we met?

He rubbed his mouth more firmly against my own, making my skin tingle.

His fingers threaded through my hair, drawing me even closer. So close.

I kissed him. Opened my mouth for his tongue, tasted him, and craved him like I'd never wanted anything in my life.

He was like a drug to my senses. A languorous melting of my body and mind, making me soften to the hands roaming my back, molding my body against his.

The hardness of him nudged against me. Firm. Hot. And throbbing.

I want him. Wanted him so badly. Now, here.

My ass hit the edge of the kitchen table. Hands lifted me, seated me atop it. As our tongues dueled, he pushed his body between my thighs, and I was tearing at his shirt. Hands skimmed over clothing then under to touch flesh. I sucked his tongue. I wanted to suck something else.

Hell, I wanted his mouth sucking on me.

My hands were on the belt for his pants—

Bong. Bong. Bong. Twelve times it rang. Twelve times, the witching hour. Enough times to cool my ardor and remind me of who I kissed.

A stranger. An enigma. A wizard. Possibly something else.

What am I doing?

Without a word, I slipped from his grasp and went to bed.

Alone.

And I won't lie and say I wasn't disappointed when he didn't try to follow me.

Chapter Nineteen

Has a woman ever walked away from me before? Alistair couldn't recall it ever happening. The novelty of it did nothing for his aching cock.

If he'd wondered at their compatibility before, he didn't now. The fiery passion that had erupted between them didn't care about the case or so-called notions of proper relationships.

Wizard, witch, sorceress. The needs of the body demanded fulfillment. He knew she felt it, too. Sensed it.

Yet she'd walked away.

Didn't even say goodnight or offer him a blanket.

Did she want him to chase after?

A man had his pride. He wouldn't go without invitation. Let her come to him. In the meantime, he'd get some sleep. He had a feeling he wouldn't be getting much soon.

He quickly discovered that there was no extra bed in her home; the spare bedroom had been converted into a greenhouse space redolent with the smell of growing green things and earth. The other room had been made into a lab.

As for the basement? He didn't do below-ground quarters. It reminded him too much of home—and not in a good way.

He took the couch, the lumpy, uncomfortable couch.

I should be sleeping with her. How else to keep an eye on her?

Don't you mean put your hands on her? He'd bet she felt soft.

There will be no touching. No more allowing himself to be distracted from his primary purpose. From this point on, he would remain clear-headed—and blue-balled.

To divert his mind from what she might be wearing, he thought about what he'd learned. Which still led him back to Willow and the fact that there was more than met the eye.

Her whole family had something off about them. None of them were what they seemed, and he wondered how that had slipped everyone's or, most specifically, TDCM's attention.

According to public records, Ann and her husband, Willum, were human. The research he'd done on Willow had her descended from parents who barely tested with magic at all. Dad was just a regular Joe who did car repair. When he retired from the garage he'd built into a business, two of his sons took over.

The other four chose other paths.

None of them were official witches. Nothing on paper anyhow, although Willow did admit that they studied sorcery.

Who did they work for? Willow wouldn't say. Did another secret agency exist out there, one that even the TDCM was ignorant about? Alistair hated being in the dark.

Then there was the mother, a blank slate who, on the surface, appeared human. Too human, which was the problem. How did she hide her power?

He might never have known if Willow had not admitted that her mom was the real power in the family. Which made sense. Seven kids didn't spontaneously inherit magic without at least one parent having it, and apparently, it was generational. A strong bloodline to have managed to keep sorcery alive—and hidden—for this long.

We all have secrets. Especially Alistair. Willow had begun unraveling his. She'd discovered that he wasn't the true son of Fitzroy. The demon attack might have distracted her from that fact, but she wouldn't let it rest.

He expected that by morning, after a night's rest, she'd be prying, chipping at his carefully created persona.

What would he tell her? The truth still wasn't an option. Yet, he had to tell her something. Just like he couldn't have her spilling his secrets. If she told someone at the TDCM…it could ruin so many things.

So kill her. Usually, he wouldn't hesitate. The mission was more important than one woman. Meant more than a hundred human women.

But he couldn't bring himself to do it. Surely, he could make her understand he had his reasons. Get her to trust him.

Why am I agonizing over this? It was rather emasculating the way she'd twisted his goals, and she didn't even grasp the depths of how much she affected him, or else she wouldn't be in her bed.

Alone.

He turned on the couch. It creaked, protesting the abuse by his big and heavy body. He'd probably wreck it if he spent the night on it.

He couldn't leave, though. Not with all the attacks. Were they only aimed at him? Alistair's mission made him a target, but what of the obvious interest in Willow? Was it simply guilt by association?

If he left, would they leave her alone? What if he left and they attacked, and Alistair wasn't there to defend her?

Best not risk it. Besides, she'd proven useful thus far.

She'd be even more useful naked.

What did she sleep in? The other night when he'd come at her call, she'd worn ridiculous nightwear that covered her neck to ankle. She still looked fetching.

Did she perhaps wear something with a little less fabric knowing he was here? Did she toss and turn like he did, unable to settle her mind? Kept awake by the needs of her body…

He stared at the dark hall leading to her bedroom. So near, and yet so far. How long would it take to reach her if something tried to break in? Would he even hear an attack?

He twiddled his thumbs.

The house creaked.

Normal shifting.

The house rattled as a plane passed

overhead.

He sighed.

Hold on, did he hear something from the bedroom?

Better check it out.

Getting to his feet, he left the top button of his pants undone, and his shirt remained on the armrest of the couch. He padded down the hall to the closed door that taunted him. The knob turned at this touch.

Years of stealthy practice meant he entered without making noise. The game of stealth being the first every child he knew learned. Everything growing up was a trial, a test of skills, a way to get extra food or praise.

Given his upbringing, he'd expected a spell to hit as soon as he crossed the bedroom threshold, so he had a shield ready. However, nothing happened.

He entered and saw a woman-sized lump under a flowery comforter. It didn't move, not even when he stood over her. A gaze down at her peaceful features showed Willow slept.

How could she sleep with the turmoil she'd left him in?

Alistair paced around her room, not a large space, a queen-sized bed and two nightstands wide. The carpet underfoot cradled his bare feet with thick fibers. The curtains hanging over the windows appeared to be of the blackout kind. The only light came from a plug-in on the wall, a softly glowing crescent moon highlighting a witch-on-a-broom silhouette.

He stood by her bedside, unabashedly staring.

How peaceful she appeared, her lashes resting against the tops of her cheeks. Her lips slightly parted.

Why does she fascinate me so much? He'd met more beautiful women. More socially acceptable ones, too. He knew women who didn't argue. Who wouldn't shove away if he kissed them.

So, why her?

"You're being creepy."

The words startled him, especially since he realized he'd fallen for her opossum act. "I was checking on something."

"I'm not naked under these blankets if that's what you're wondering."

One illusion shattered. "I thought I heard something."

"You mean the sound of your ego deflating because I didn't let you into my pants?"

She rolled onto her back, and despite the gloom of the room, he could see her staring at him.

"You were right to push me away. You are a distraction I can ill afford."

"Is that because you're an imposter?" She shoved herself to a seated position, the comforter falling to her waist and showing off her T-shirt that said, *Warning: Witch with Attitude.*

"I'm not your enemy."

"Says you, but I only have your word for that. Who are you? Really? Are you even a wizard like you say?"

He held up his hands, letting a tiny ball of

light dance between the palms. "You've seen me do magic."

"Which we both know doesn't mean shit. I do magic, too, and I'm not a wizard."

The boldness of her words, not to mention the intelligence, spurred him to speak, and reveal. "What if I were to tell you that there are races in the world that even the TDCM knows nothing about? Some so well hidden that their very existence doesn't appear in any historical annals." Because no one wanted a reminder of the past.

Her lips pursed. "Is that what you're claiming to be? Some unknown mysterious species with magic and a big nose meddling in our affairs?"

"My nose isn't big." Other parts of him were, however.

"I don't see you denying the meddling."

"I wouldn't exactly call it that."

"What, then? Spying?"

"Of a sort."

She scrambled to her knees, and her expression turned fierce. "You're a traitor."

"Before you try to turn me in, listen. My infiltration of the TDCM might have been under falsified pretenses. However, it was the most efficient way to get my hands on the information I need."

"Need for what?"

"I am not at liberty to say."

But she knew. Guessed immediately. "This is about the demons."

A direct lie would serve no purpose. "Yes."

"Are you a demon?"

"No." Not in the sense she believed anyway.

"But you know of them."

"Yes, and I can tell you that they are a bad thing to have happen to the world."

"So what's your plan to deal with them? Because, I assume, you do have one and aren't just dicking us all around for shits and giggles."

"I cannot say more on the matter. Suffice it to say, there are those looking into the situation." Some who wanted to act before it was too late, as opposed to those who decided to ignore the plight of mankind and the world.

"I should turn you in," she said, a frown wrinkling her brow. "But then that would mean working with Morfeus or some other asshat at the TDCM."

"Does this mean I'm not an asshat?" His lips quirked.

"Oh, you're still a jerk, but at least you're tolerable."

"Only tolerable? I would have thought I was more than that."

"Why would you think that?" She arched a brow. "Because I kissed you? I've kissed plenty of men."

For some reason, the boast fired something inside him, brought out a savage possessiveness, and he growled, "None of them can compare to me."

"If you say so," spoken with a smirk.

The mockery couldn't be borne. The ache in his loins needed relief. The fire in his blood…only she could quench it.

He grabbed her by the upper arms, and she sucked in a breath, her vivid eyes locked on his. She didn't struggle as he muttered, "Why must you constantly argue?"

"Because I can't allow myself to like you," was her whispered reply.

"Would that be so bad?"

"We're not compatible."

Really? Tell that to the molten desire running through his body. "I'd say the problem is"—he brushed his lips softly across the skin of her cheek, barely touching—"that we are too much in tune."

"We can't do this. Shouldn't," she said, her eyelids drooping, her head tilting back.

"Too late," he murmured. *I can't stop myself.* He slanted his mouth over hers, claiming her lips, tasting her.

It ignited the passion that had been simmering between them. They went from verbally sparring and dancing around their desire to locked in a frantic kiss.

He lost all reason in that moment. Forgot all the reasons why they shouldn't be doing this. Forgot he should be watching for danger. Keeping his distance.

But doing so meant not holding her in his arms and tasting the sweetness of her lips.

Arousal washed over him, and awash in sensation, every nerve ending in his body alive, he nibbled at her lips and, when she parted them, sucked on her tongue.

Despite her protests, she didn't try to escape. On the contrary, she gripped him tightly, fingers digging into his shoulders.

His mouth left the sweet haven of her mouth to drag along the skin of her jaw to her ear.

A soft moan escaped her, and her hands slid into his hair, yanking it, pulling him back. "We should stop," she said.

"Do you really want me to stop?" he growled. He stared at her, her lids heavy with languor.

She wet her lips. "No. No, I don't."

The answer he needed. He crushed his mouth to hers, and his hands skimmed over her shirt, finding the hem and sliding under to touch bare and smooth flesh.

Not to be outdone, she caressed the bare skin of his back, branding him with her palms, bringing him alive in a way he'd never experienced.

Usually a man in control, he felt awash in sensation. Propelled by desire and need.

Her shirt came off, leaving her bared to him. Her hands found the zipper to his pants and took care of it, shoving them down, denuding him.

Flesh-to-flesh contact drew a groan from him. Her curves felt so right against him.

He pulled back, far enough that he could see her, admire her full hips, slightly curved belly, and perfect handfuls of breasts. A body made to worship, especially the puckered nipples.

As he admired her, so did she ogle him, and his cock, already hard, managed to achieve a steel-like quality.

"Damn," she whispered.

A word that made him growl, "Come here." Hooking her by the nape, he dragged her to him and devoured her mouth. She nipped his lip, and he made a noise.

He wanted her so badly.

But first, a taste of her berries. His mouth slid down her neck, past the rapid flutter of her pulse, then farther still to her breasts. He couldn't help but cup them as he teased the flesh, weighing them in his hands, squeezing them.

"They're not melons," she said with a soft chuckle.

"Yet I bet they taste delicious," was his reply before latching on to a pert nipple.

She cried out as he sucked, guttural noises of desire. She yanked his hair, demanding more, unafraid to show her pleasure.

He shoved her back onto the bed, lying her upon it, legs splayed. He knelt between her thighs, cock jutting proudly.

She eyed him, eyes soft with arousal, wet lips parted. She crooked a finger and beckoned him.

Surely she didn't mean…

She beckoned again, and he groaned.

"I don't think—"

"Don't think." She reached out, and he moved closer. She reached for him.

What man could resist?

He moved close enough to give her what she asked for.

Her lips latched on to his swollen head.

Damn. He threw his head back and uttered a sound then shuddered as she drew him deeper into her mouth, suctioning him. While her mouth lavished attention on his length, her fingers kneaded his sac. She paid wet attention to every inch of him, sliding him in and out, bobbing her head along his length, fast and eager.

Despite her needing no urging, he still weaved his fingers into her hair, tugging it hard enough to make her growl, the sound vibrating along the length of his cock.

It almost made him come.

Not yet. It was too soon. He hadn't had his turn.

He pulled free, and she made a sound of protest, her lips not ready to relinquish their prize.

"My turn," he growled, positioning himself between her thighs.

The scent of her enveloped him, and he wasted no time going in for a lick. He let his agile tongue flick across her clit, teasing the nub, making it swell.

He nipped it, pulling it with his lips while she bucked under him, panting and mewling. Her fingers dug into the sheets as she went wild under his attentions.

But he wanted her more than wild. He wanted her to come.

One finger. Two. He thrust them into her, feeling her moist channel pulsing around them as his tongue worked her button. He pushed deep and was rewarded with a sharp cry and a shudder as her first orgasm hit.

Her flesh shivered around his fingers, and she gasped for breath.

He didn't stop. Even as she mewled, "It's too much," he held her down and kept going until she began moaning and crying out, "Yes, yes."

That was his cue. He covered her body with his, inserting himself between her thighs, the tip of his shaft probing her moist sex.

He thrust, hard and deep jabs that had her panting.

Not good enough. He grabbed her by the ass and changed his angle of entry and thrust again.

A sharp cry met him, and her body clenched.

Found her sweet spot.

He began to pump her, over and over, striking her G-spot each time, leaving her unable to catch her breath.

Yet she still found enough air to let loose a window-shaking scream as her second climax ripped through her. A major orgasm that fisted his cock, and brought him close to her, so close, their magic, wild in that moment of uncontrolled passion, touched and exploded.

He bellowed her name as he came, hot spurts that marked her womb. A joining of bodies unlike anything he'd ever experienced or imagined.

Fucking perfection.

At least he thought it was. Willow, on the other hand...

"You idiot!" She shoved at him, and her eyes blazed.

"What's wrong?" He truly didn't grasp the

problem. She'd orgasmed, twice. The tiny quivers of her flesh still rippled around him.

"You came inside me."

Yes, he most certainly had.

Made her mine. Which caused him to feel great satisfaction.

But according to the ire sparking in her eyes, she was most definitely not happy about it.

Chapter Twenty

"I can't believe you did that," I snapped, my body relaxed and blissful in the aftermath of some epic orgasms but my mind shocked and dismayed.

"What did you expect would happen?" was his sarcastic reply. "Or did you plan for this to be one-sided?"

"Of course, I didn't. But did you have to come inside me? Would it have killed you to stop and grab a condom?"

"I didn't see you pausing the action."

"I was kind of busy," I yelled in reply. Busy coming so hard I almost believed in Heaven.

"Well, so was I."

How dare he have so much fun he forgot the important stuff? "You should have pulled out."

"Are you really going to blame me when it's your fault for making it feel so damned good?"

Ooh, I almost melted there. "Just because I'm epic, it isn't an excuse to not practice safe sex."

"I don't see what the problem is. If you're worried about disease, I'm clean."

"Says you. And what about pregnancy?"

"Aren't you on birth control?"

"No." Because the damned hormone pills screwed with my magic. "Please tell me whatever you are isn't compatible with me." I begged him for reassurance, even as my mind conjured up cute little blond-haired babies with his eyes.

"We're compatible. But I doubt it will happen after just one time."

"Said every man before accidentally becoming a daddy." I rolled my eyes and shoved at him.

He moved, taking his heat with him, removing his delicious weight, and I immediately regretted it.

My wanton body wanted to stay snuggled. I, on the other hand, was going to hop in a shower and aim the spray at my girly parts and hope I didn't miss my next period. Despite what my mother wanted, I wasn't ready for kids.

Mostly because I haven't found the right guy.

I cast a glance at Alistair lying on my bed, looking too comfortable. *Or have I?*

Mental slap. Now was not the time to be thinking of him as a potential boyfriend. We were supposed to be working together on a dire problem, not fucking.

But it was epic fucking.

That would never happen again.

As I showered, I listed to myself all the reasons why it wouldn't work.

It was a pretty good list.

1. I don't know what he is. Not quite human. Not an elf. What did that leave?
2. He's a wizard.
3. Arrogant and cocky.

4.   My family would never accept him. And I thought this despite the almost successful dinner party.

5.   No room in my closet.

Lots of valid reasons, and the only argument for us hooking up?

I like him.

Like wasn't enough.

Emerging from the bathroom wrapped in a huge towel, I found him on his phone, his voice low, his conversation halting the moment I entered the room.

"Has there been another incident?" I asked.

"Nothing that requires urgent attention."

"So no bodies?"

He shook his head, and my shoulders relaxed. "I'll call you back in a bit." He tucked the phone into the pants he'd pulled on. Guess he wasn't making an attempt at round two.

Not that I would have allowed it, of course. Hello, I had a list!

One that wouldn't last long if he kept staring at me, his eyes smoldering with heat, pricking me between the legs. "You should go."

"I thought we argued earlier about this. I'm staying here to protect you."

"What about the phone call?"

His brow knit. "They'll have to wait until sunrise. Unless you wish to join me."

"More demons?"

"Not exactly, a problem at the bureau headquarters. Something about an artifact. You could stay in my office while I deal with it."

"So you can stash away your embarrassment?" I snapped.

"Do you really believe I am embarrassed by you?"

"You're a wizard, remember? I know you are."

"Perhaps I should stay here and show you how wrong you are."

"Yeah, about that." I would have whistled innocently if I knew how. "I might have kind of made a phone call before I showered."

His gaze narrowed. "To who?"

"My brothers. Banyan and Ash are coming over to watch me. I should probably mention that they take their job of protecting me very seriously. As in, if they discover you seduced me, you might find yourself with your head up your ass." They had this thing about boys messing with their little sister.

"Your brothers don't scare me."

I cocked my head. "Maybe they don't, but let me make something clear. Hurt them, and I will hurt you."

His eyes turned flat, and his nostrils flared. "You aren't playing fair."

"Get used to it."

A ghost of a grin pulled at his lips. "You can't chase me off so easily, Willow. There is something between us."

"You're right. There is something between us. Centuries of tradition. Your secrets. The demons." I shook my head. "It would never work."

"Worked just fine a short while ago," he said, his gaze roving over my body.

Way to sucker-punch me in the cunt. "The sex is good, I'll grant you that, but I don't trust you."

"You should trust that I won't hurt you."

"Again, said every man before doing the exact opposite. This argument is not going anywhere. I am not changing my mind. You need to leave."

I thought for sure he'd argue again. Maybe try and sway me with his mouth and hands. My body tingled in anticipation. Instead, Alistair grabbed his shirt and covered his body. "I'll go, but you won't get rid of me so easily."

"Obviously, considering we still have the case to work on, but this"—I pointed to me, him, and the rumpled bed—"that's done."

Said with conviction, yet as soon as he left, I felt deflated.

He didn't even fight that hard to stay. Not even a single kiss to show me how wrong I was.

Jerk.

My annoyance with him probably explained my terse attitude with my brothers when they arrived, and the restless sleep I got that night.

The next morning, my gritty eyes glared at my cheerful siblings where they sat at my table devouring a month's worth of groceries.

"You'd better be planning to replace that," I grumbled as I made myself a cup of coffee.

"Someone is on her period," Oak muttered.

"Am not."

"Then your crabby attitude must be because of that wizard you're working with. Want me to beat him up for you?" Banyan offered before inhaling a loaf of toasted bread.

"I don't need your help with Alistair."

"And she doesn't deny he's the problem!" Oak chortled. "She's got a thing for a wizard." The words were sung, and my mighty glare didn't ignite him on the spot.

"Watch it, or I'll tell Mother you're the one who broke her grandmother's Royal Doulton."

His eyes narrowed. "You wouldn't dare."

"Don't piss me off."

"Someone needs to get laid," Banyan rumbled.

Actually, that was my problem. I'd gotten laid. Liked it, and wanted more.

What was wrong with me?

"So look what I found wandering around your yard this morning." Oak reached under the table into his lap and pulled out an orange bundle of fur.

"Whiskers!" I yelled, diving for my kitten.

My baby kitty meowed at the sight of me and lifted a paw. I nestled him in my arms, trying not to squish him—not easy because I wanted to hug him and love him and squeeze him. I was so happy he'd come back instead of being digested inside some demon's stomach.

Then I had a horrifying thought.

What if Whiskers had been taken over by a demon like those other pets had?

I held him up to eye level and peered at

him. Peeked at his aura, simple and orange. Sniffed him. Smelled liked wet grass and kitty.

How could I tell if it was my baby?

The furball opened one sleepy eye and yawned. He blinked open both eyes and began to purr. An aircraft-carrier-loud rumble as he showed his happiness at seeing me.

Awwww. I snuggled him close. Perhaps my love life was a mess, but at least my cat was back.

With daylight making everything bright, I felt no qualms about kicking out my brothers. Kal would be arriving shortly, and besides, only an idiot would attack me in my home.

A witch's house was her haven. A sorceress's house was her fortress. With the mood I found myself in, I'd have welcomed a distraction. Alas, not even a salesman tried to disturb my peace.

On my third cup of coffee and wading through emails, Kal arrived, one of the few people keyed into my place and allowed entry.

With a, "Morning, boss," he entered the kitchen and caused me to blink.

He'd chosen a rather eye-popping yellow shirt with snug, dark slacks paired with a multi-hued scarf and aviator glasses today.

"You look like shit," he announced upon seeing me.

"Says the man who swallowed the sun. Would it kill you to turn down the brightness a notch?"

"Spoken by a woman wearing a T-shirt that would look better in a rubbish bin."

That earned him a finger. I was rather fond of my T-shirts. Every year for Christmas, my brothers found me a new one, something tacky with a ridiculous saying about witches. This one stated, *Bitchcraft*.

Kal didn't heed the subtle warning on my chest. "Someone needs to snap out of her funk. Especially since we have to go shopping today."

"Shopping?" I wrinkled my nose. "Like hell. We have work to do." Such as lying on the couch and working on a nap.

"No shopping? Then I guess you're not hitting the ball tomorrow, after all."

"Is that already here?" I'd lost track of time, apparently. I was pretty sure I could blame Alistair for that, too.

"It is here, and unless you're planning to wear something from last year"—not too likely since I'd spilled wine on it—"then we need to get you something that fits off the rack."

"But I don't want to go shopping. I've got work to do. People to call."

"We can make those calls on the way there, and while you're trying on gowns, I can fire off texts to those who've yet to reply. Now, go get dressed and do something about your hair."

"I hate you," I grumbled.

"Good, then that means I'm doing my job as your assistant," Kal riposted.

Thank goodness for efficient employees. While my brain still felt sluggish, and my thoughts were chaotic, Kal managed to get me organized and out the door.

The addition of food to my caffeine belly restored me somewhat so that, by the time we hit the dress shop, I almost felt human. Human enough that I wondered what Alistair was up to.

Where did he go last night?
Where is he now?
Why hasn't he called?
Will he call?

No wonder I couldn't sleep.

Being clueless when it came to style, I put myself in Kal's hands at the dress shop. He knew a posh one that boasted enough styles and sizes to torture me. While he took up a spot outside a changing room, I tried on dresses.

And more dresses. Then more after that.

The problem with having an assistant who knew about style was that I didn't get away with trying on just one.

I got to enjoy a short commentary as I emerged in frock after frock.

"Too short."

"Too frilly."

"Beads?" That one got a snort.

"Bows don't belong on any gown."

Criticism after criticism until I emerged in one that Kal declared, "Just right."

"Are you sure?" I asked, twirling to view it from all angles in the mirror.

The mauve number was bold. So very, very bold. And sexy. It hugged my curves from my neck where it had a band across my throat, over my breasts, where a strategically placed hole showed some cleavage, then down to where it nipped into my waist and then flared out over hips.

I looked like…

"A goddess." Kal clapped his hands. "About time you wore something to showcase your gifts."

"I hardly call having thirty-six D boobs gifts." He'd obviously never tried to jump on a trampoline with them.

"You will turn heads in that number."

Did I want to draw attention?

I looked at myself in the mirror, a voluptuous redhead in an eye-popping gown that screamed, "look at me."

It's time. Time to stop hiding. Time to stop pretending to be something I wasn't.

I knew what the coven recommended. It wanted the sorcerers among them to remain hidden, to not let anyone know that humans had magic, powers on par with the other races.

Why? Why did we have to hide who we were?

Witches and sorcerers alike deserved respect. This wasn't the Dark Ages. We wouldn't allow ourselves to be hung and tortured in the name of a false religion as part of the agenda of the wizards.

The time had come for us to be accepted as equals.

And, as an equal, I could date a wizard.

Make Alistair my boyfriend.

Even have his damned babies if I so chose.

The question was, did I dare upset centuries of order?

Screw letting rules and other people decide what I could have or who I could be.

The only person who should be making decisions about my life was me. If I wanted a certain man, not just any man, a wizard who was my equal and more, then dammit, I should be allowed to have him.

As I gave one last twirl of my dress, I smiled. *Wait until Alistair sees me in this.*

Despite what he'd done, I couldn't stay mad at the man who made my toes curl. The one who'd finally texted me.

It wasn't a flowery speech.

What are you doing?

Feeling somewhat mischievous, blame it on the dress, I texted back.

Looking incredibly sexy.

His reply?

You always look sexy.

More than my toes curled.

What do you want? Do we have a break in the case?

Come to headquarters. I want to show you something in the vault.

Hello, had Alistair seriously just invited me to peek inside the wizard's secret vault?

That was a big deal. I wondered if Morfeus would be there with his lemon-sucking face for me to take a picture.

I'll be there in half an hour.

Long enough to pay for my dress, drop off Kal, and then whip over there.

I could hardly contain my giddiness, and it

wasn't just because I'd been invited into the inner sanctum. I'd get to see Alistair.

Don't be too eager. Alistair needed to recognize that he didn't call the shots. Plus, I was still mad about the whole no-condom thing.

Which might have been why I detoured a few minutes and purchased a special anti-fertility amulet on the way over.

Not that I planned to have sex with him again.

Snicker. Even I didn't believe that lie.

Chapter Twenty-one

She's coming. Emasculating himself, Alistair had been the first to initiate contact. He'd had to because, as the hours passed without her around, he'd gotten antsy.

He didn't understand it. Couldn't fight it. He'd tried to walk away the previous night after seeing her brothers arrive and setting some extra wards around her place.

Wards that wouldn't have been necessary had she allowed him to stay.

He still couldn't believe Willow had tossed him out. Was the thought of bearing his child so repugnant?

Since when did he even think of forging a family?

He blamed Willow for that. The damned woman consumed his thoughts, and it didn't help that when they were apart, he worried.

It didn't matter that she was strong or had her brothers with her. No one was as good as Alistair.

Now if only she realized it, too. Of course, for her to recognize his greatness, she'd actually have to be in his presence. It took dangling the right carrot for her to agree to meet him at the office.

On his way to meet her at reception, Morfeus thought to waylay him in the halls, but Alistair wasn't in the mood.

"I'm busy," he snapped, not slowing his steps.

"I need to speak with you." Morfeus kept pace with Alistair.

"Do you have new information for me?" he bit out. When it came to Morfeus, he found himself imbued with a heavy dislike. Something about the wizard grated.

"I am here to serve the right hand in any way he needs."

The words stopped him dead. He turned to look at Morfeus. "What did you say?"

"I am at your disposal. I know of the plan and am honored to have been chosen to be part of it."

This about-face in attitude saw Alistair drawing Morfeus into a room. He shut the door before asking, "What do you know? Who have you spoken to?"

"I know everything. Someone came to speak to me and showed me the way." A fanatical light gleamed in his eyes. "The legion is only here to cleanse the world of the impure ones. To once again make it the oasis it was meant to be for the true races."

Someone had most certainly gotten to Morfeus. Alistair scrubbed at his face. "Who else knows?"

"No one. They wouldn't understand." The

slyness in his eyes held a hint of smug madness.

"Keep it a secret." Because if word emerged of what was to come…wide-spread panic would follow.

"Tell me what you need. I am your servant."

The words sounded sincere, such a change from the pompous ones of before.

"I need you to not get in my way." Things were heading to a point. He couldn't be one hundred percent sure, but he was convinced the dimensions were almost perfectly aligned.

Soon, chaos would enter this world.

Conquer and destroy it like it had the one before.

There were too few standing against that plight.

So little time before perhaps all was lost.

Precious little time left with Willow.

He glanced at his watch and cursed. "I need to go. Tell no one," he ordered Morfeus.

He had to get to Willow because, while he might have invited her to visit, he doubted anyone would let her in. And that would make her mad.

Chapter Twenty-two

Only as I stood in front of the nondescript headquarters of the TDCM did I regret it.

I shouldn't have come. They'd never let me in to see inside their precious vault. It had been made clear to me countless times that a hearth witch wasn't good enough to set foot inside their inner sanctum.

But I want to see the mysterious parchment Alistair told me about.

Lie. *Admit it, you didn't come to see a piece of paper. You came to see Alistair.*

Had I really talked myself into believing we could have something more than great sex? A chasm stretched between us. One I didn't know if I could, or even should, cross. As a sorceress, I shouldn't exist. I might be his equal, but the world didn't know that. The wizards would never accept that.

A relationship, even the hint of one, was a distraction I didn't need right now.

A fork in my life had arrived. I could see it looming in front of me. On the one branch, I had the choice of remaining in hiding. Being a good little witch who didn't rock the broom.

The other road had me declaring my status

as sorceress and a wizard's equal. Not disguising my true abilities.

A chance to be me.

But there was one glaring issue with my coming out. Perhaps I was ready to reveal myself, but what of the other sorcerers? Did I have the right to make that choice for them?

A part of me wanted to scream, "It's my life, too, I should get to choose," but I couldn't be a total selfish bitch and make that choice for those who were happy hiding.

A conundrum with no resolution.

I sighed as I looked in front of me at the worn concrete steps into the nondescript TDCM building. The metal handrail embedded in the stairs, chipped in places where the paint had peeled from age—and cheapness. The TDCM saw no reason to pretty up the exterior of their building. They were about not drawing attention.

So much hiding. What would really happen if the world knew magic, *real* magic, existed?

The humans had dealt well—better than anticipated—with the emergence of other species. Sure, there'd been some violence. You kind of had to expect it. The world wasn't a perfect place, not even always a nice one. However, at the core, the majority of people were good.

If that were the case, then why was I afraid?

Despite the battle going on within, my feet moved of their own accord. The front door to the building yielded to my touch. An electrical shock skimmed over my body and skin, a spell meant to check me out.

One of hundreds humanity remained ignorant of.

Can you imagine the industries that could be built if magic worked openly with science? Why didn't that possibility alone make it viable for magic to admit its presence?

I could make a fortune openly selling my hangover cures and the one that grew thick lashes.

Thinking about stupid things helped me ignore the fact that I'd stepped inside.

The lure of the vault pulled me, but the bigger magnet remained Alistair. I couldn't stay away.

Chin held high, I strutted like I belonged. I wore heels today—the thick and clomping kind. The type that said, "you can't pretend you don't hear me coming."

The fellow at the desk was the same snotty bastard as before. He kept his nose bent, deliberately pretending he didn't hear the horse-trot cadence striking the tile.

I didn't wait for him to look up. "Grande Mago Fitzroy is expecting me," I declared. I skipped the niceties. Nice hadn't worked last time, and he was already pissing me off.

"Wait your turn."

I blinked. Wait for whom? I stood alone in front of the desk.

Was Snooty on the phone? His ears appeared bare of listening devices. No sign of a phone, not even a cellular kind. Add to that the fact that he didn't converse aloud with anyone.

There was no one here. Did that mean he

talked to someone in his mind?

Mother had raised me not to be rude. What if he did talk to someone I couldn't see or hear?

Then why did he scroll on his tablet, stopping on an image in some social media timeline?

Oh, hell no. I slapped my hand down on his desk. "Oh, you do not want to be screwing with me today."

He lifted a bored—and slightly sneering—countenance. "Wait your turn. *Witch.*"

"You shouldn't have said that." I shook my head and tsked. I drew on some magic, just a little so as not to set off any alarms, and clenched my fist, grasping invisible fabric and lifting it.

The snotty receptionist gasped. "What are you doing?"

"She is putting you down," boomed a voice, hinting of laughter.

I turned to see Alistair, looking dashing as always in a fresh pair of slacks and another of those V-necked shirts.

Damn, he looked good in those.

"Why should I put him down?" I gave him a little shake. "He's an annoying twat who can't even muster enough magic to pry one of my fingers loose. This is what passes for a wizard?"

It was kind of pathetic. I knew plenty of so-called witches who didn't even try for higher sorceress magic who had more power than this. And we were considered inferior?

"The college standards have seemingly been lowered. The specimens coming out of them lately are definitely not on par with previous generations."

"I'm plenty strong in magic," blustered the asshat. "I'm just not supposed to use it in public."

I snickered. "Is that really what you're going with?" A little shake up and down had him screeching with terror. He probably didn't do amusement parks, given his low threshold for adventure.

Alistair tried to hide a smile. "Put the wizard down."

"But what if I want to keep him as a pet?" Baring my teeth had the lovely effect of making Snotty blanch.

"He'd make a piss-poor pet. I've got something more interesting. Come see the parchment I told you about." Alistair held out his hand.

I eyed it suspiciously. I knew what that hand was capable of. Touching me and making me want things. It also brought extreme pleasure, as did other parts of him.

My gaze strayed, and his voice dropped an octave when he repeated, "Come with me, Willow."

Yes. Yes, I wanted to come.

And I meant it as dirty as it sounded.

I opened my fist and let the twerp drop. He hit his chair. The armrest held, but I wasn't sure if his ribs did. The good news for him? He had access to healers so he wouldn't be whining for long.

I, on the other hand, had just attacked a

wizard. At least that was how they'd see it. Never mind the snot had asked for it. I, a lowly witch, had dared to lay a magical hand on one of them.

Something they'd question.

I'll have to tell them I'm a sorceress. I'd have to divulge my secret. *Look at that, I made a decision.*

The world would just have to live with it.

I stepped toward Alistair, his hand still outstretched.

Don't take it. I'm still mad. The man had totally played me the night before. Coming into my bedroom. Looking ridiculously sexy. Was it any wonder we had mind-blowing sex?

Exactly why was I mad at him again?

My fingers reached out and laced through his. A public display of affection between a wizard and a supposed witch.

The TDCM didn't collapse in horror.

A tingle went through me as he tightened his grip and drew me closer. "Are you always connected to trouble?"

"As much as possible. It keeps me looking young."

At that, he barked in laughter, the sound deep and rich. "You are fascinating."

"Thanks." What else could I say when my insides turned to warm putty? I mean, seriously, when a man said he found you fascinating in a seriously hot and low voice… Total melting of parts.

He kept hold of my hand as we walked through the halls. Did he fear I'd run off?

Maybe he wants to hold my hand. I certainly

enjoyed it. Say what you would, there was something intimate about the gesture. Something that said, "mine."

It caused more than a few curious looks as we passed people in the halls. Some sneered. Others managed disdain. I kept my chin high.

I am just as strong as most of you. I deserve to be here.

"Don't worry," Alistair murmured.

"Let me guess," I muttered. "You'll protect me." How like a guy to assume I needed help. My father and brothers were the same way.

"Don't tell me you're too lazy to care for yourself all of a sudden?" he teased.

"No."

"Good. I was talking more about being worried about the parchment."

Hunh? "Never even entered my mind. Why would I be scared?"

"Um, you haven't heard what happened."

"Not exactly…what happened?" As if he could leave me hanging.

"Some people who looked at it were adversely affected."

Like pulling teeth. "Affected how?"

He paused before a wall made of white marble, inset with a small door. As soon as he tapped it with a finger, the entire wall and door lit up like a Christmas tree on steroids.

"What the hell? Those are some serious wards." I'd never seen the like. Patterns crisscrossing. Sigils. Symbols. Layers of magic woven in, with so many different signatures.

Alistair gestured. "This is the vault." Almost said with an ominous dum-dum-dum. "It protects and hides some of the more unbalanced magic the TDCM has come across."

"Unbalanced in what sense?" I asked, eyeing the seeming overkill of protection at the door. What could be so awful that they had to seal it so ridiculously?

"For lack of a better way to put it, there is good and evil in the world. Some things out there help make lives better, easier. Happier, too. Then there are things that don't. Things that curse people with death, madness, disease."

"Is that paper one of those cursed things?"

"Only to the weak-minded. So you should be fine." He grinned, wide and so handsome my heart skipped a beat.

"*Should be* fine is not reassuring."

"Don't tell me you're afraid?"

I feared many things, like what the man in front of me might mean to my future, but a tiny piece of paper? "I'm not scared."

"Good." Alistair moved to the little door, and it was then that I realized the statues of two wizards in ancient armor weren't statues at all.

Heads covered in helms, their robes a thick woven material that glinted like metal, they held long blades. The lengthy, wooden hilts were polished smooth with only a hint of writing on the sanded surfaces. Script that glowed.

"Halt and state your business," one of them stated.

"I have permission to be here."

"She doesn't," said tin can number two.

"She's with me."

The two soldiers didn't seem to care and kept their blades aimed.

I stepped closer to Alistair. "Are they going to kill me if you open that door?" I asked.

"Not unless they want to die a few seconds after. I have the full right and privilege to enter and bring whatever expert I deem necessary with me. They know better than to get in my way."

"Why are they dressed so hardcore?" I'd never seen wizards armored before except in very old pictures.

"Mostly, they're attired like this to protect themselves should they need to hold something off if it tries to exit."

"Again, not reassuring." I cast a glance over my shoulder as I stuck close to Alistair. They couldn't hit me without hitting one of their own.

"A little bit of fear only serves to fuel adrenaline. Ready?" He placed his palm on the door, and I tensed.

Oh, boy. Here we go. "Let's do it."

Anticipation had me vibrating.

The door swung open, and nothing whipped out. Not even a tentacle.

I let go of a breath. One possibility I'd seen in a movie down, like a hundred to go. My vivid imagination had so many possible scenarios.

I expected something to fall on us walking through, so I let Alistair enter first. When he wasn't crushed by stone, or screaming just inside the door, punctured by poisoned arrows, I stepped in.

I didn't open my scrunched eyes until I realized nothing killed me. That eased my shoulders a bit more.

The expression on his face, wary and tense, tightened them again.

"Don't touch anything," Alistair warned. "Some of the things in here are dangerous."

Some of them? The waves of energy, a lot of it malevolent in feeling, some of it slimy, washed over me in discordant jangles. Think of several choirs trying to sing completely different songs and nothing in rhythm. It was noise. Magical dissonance that dulled the senses.

"This is awful," I said. "Whose bright idea was it to put all of this shit in one spot? I mean, you've got all you need for an Armageddon right here."

"Which is why it's in here. These pieces can subvert whoever has them in his or her possession. Compare it to a seductive siren song. But when too many sirens sing, the spell is interrupted. You can think, albeit with a bit of pain."

"A bit. You'd better have something to fix my headache." Only when he tossed me a very teasing grin did I realize how that sounded. "I meant Tylenol."

"No need for pills. I have something better than that." And damn if a wizard couldn't purr.

"So where is this thing you want me to see?" I walked toward him, even as my gaze remained caught on a green helm, delicately balanced on the tip of a spear. It appeared made for a woman, the delicate filigree of the head covering fluted and curved.

I could raise an army. Make the world respect me. Battle for glory.

I blinked and looked away from the helmet and spear set. Focusing on a single item still had its dangers.

I almost bumped into Alistair as he stopped. His hands caught and steadied me.

"Here is the parchment."

I looked down at it. The loose brown page was lined with age yet preserved with a magical spell of lamination meant to protect. The scribbled writing looped down the page. A scrawl that took some squinting to figure out, after you got past the scrambling enchantment on it.

"It's a recipe," I announced.

"You can read it?" he exclaimed.

"Of course, I can. It was mine before it fell out of my pocket." Great-Nana's recipe for permanent hair removal. No side effects known. At all. We would make it for a song, imbue it with the needed magic, market it to women who hated shaving their legs, and be rich. Only problem was, first I'd have to find a way to get around the FDA rules.

"This is your piece of paper?" He frowned. "How come I can't read it? Or copy it? What language is this in?"

"English with shitty handwriting." Nana liked big swirls and loops. "I spelled it to be unreadable when she died, and I inherited it. Do you know how rare some spells are?" Witches and sorceresses guarded their family recipes something fierce.

"But what about the fact that some of the wizards who studied it came out babbling about voices and demons."

"My piece of paper wasn't responsible."

"Then what did it?"

Something dark tickled at me. Could Alistair not feel it...over to my right, ghostly tendrils reaching for me.

I pivoted and pointed. "That's your problem."

The innocuous horn, taken from some animal that no longer walked in our times, looked old, dried out, and slightly cracked along its brown curve. It also sizzled with energy.

Alistair walked away from me and headed to the horn, head canted to the side. "That? I don't even know why it's here. It appears to be a dud."

"No dud."

"Are you sure?" he asked with skepticism. "I sense nothing from it. Not even a slight whisper of magic."

"It might be invisible to you, but let me tell you, that thing is oozing all kinds of weird vibes."

A familiar one that reminded me of the Peabody place for some reason. But surely I was wrong. There couldn't be a portal inside the vault.

Unless an object provided an anchor point.

I stopped a few feet away from the pedestal holding the horn. Precaution wasn't something Alistair practiced. He walked right up to it, put his hand out, and touched it.

I squinted through one eye and didn't see

him blow up. Nor did he scream as if he burned.

"Still don't feel anything," he declared.

How could he not see the horn pulsing orange around his hand? It beat faster.

"I'm telling you, that horn is fucked." I brought out a stronger word to describe the rapid flashing of the horn, the orange melting into red, then green, then yellow.

"It's harmless." He waved his hand around it, and something grabbed hold and yanked.

Alistair disappeared!

Chapter Twenty-three

Nothing worse than being embarrassed in front of the woman he was courting.

And by a lowly creature.

He eyed the Ceterum, a monster he'd heard of. This was, however, the first one he'd seen.

It had a lot more tentacles than the pictures showed. And suckers on those waving arms. So much for them being extinct.

An appendage swung at his head, and Alistair ducked. Then immediately jumped over another swinging arm.

He quickly fired a bolt of fire at a third zoning in and sliced it. The tip fell off and wiggled, gray ooze eking. The creature uttered a shriek.

It could be hurt.

Cool.

The ground rumbled.

He dodged another tentacle and fired again.

Squeee. Plop.

Rumble.

Was this monster causing the tiny earthquakes?

More rumbling.

An exclaimed, "Holy shit, where are we?" had him turning his head.

"Willow?" Why had she followed?

"I think we just found a portal," she exclaimed.

Yes, they had. And it had a welcoming committee.

He fired at a tentacle that tried to hook around her ankles.

Willow's eyes widened as the limb sprayed ichor and waggled in the air.

"Um, Alistair, what is that?"

"Monster?" was his helpful reply.

"Cool." And then, as calm as a killer during times of war, she joined him in slaying the monster.

Each slice of a limb brought more and more shakes of the ground.

Not good.

He looked down at his feet.

Squee. Another limb bit the dust.

Rumble.

"Willow, I think we should get back to the vault."

She pointed at the beast. "But it's not dead."

"Yeah, and I think that's the only reason we're still alive."

Slice. Yell. Tremble.

She peeked at the ground and bit her lower lip. "That's not you doing that, is it?"

"Nope."

A mouth opened in the Ceterum's bulky body, and a fat tentacle shot out. Aimed at Willow.

Alistair didn't even hesitate. He lunged, his

arm turning into a white sword of pure magic, slicing through the tentacle with its moist suckers, severing it before those little mouths could attach to Willow.

He lay in the muck comprised of blood and dust. Silence descended. An agonizing silence as everything stilled, even the monster he'd just slain.

"Run!" he shouted, picking himself up off the ground. He ran past Willow and grabbed her by the hand, but her shoes—heels meant for looking sexy wrapped around his shoulders—didn't run very well.

When Willow stumbled, Alistair swept her into his arms. She didn't fight him but rather glanced over his shoulder and said, "Run faster."

He poured on the speed and aimed for the altar he'd spotted, half broken, its stone halves heaving skyward in the rubble. He'd wager it was linked to the horn, even if he couldn't see the magic.

"They're coming," she announced, words throaty. She didn't tremble with fear, though. Instead, she flexed her magical muscle and held out her fingers.

He couldn't see what magic she used. It certainly did nothing to curb the rumbling of the ground or quell the hisses, so many different sibilants, coming from behind them.

"It won't hold them much longer." Willow tensed in his arms, and he could feel the strain.

He leaped into the air, aiming for the spot where he hoped the rip existed.

The passage from one dimension to another

was a breath-sucking cold that spat you out into sudden warmth and left you gasping. He hit the floor on his feet but hard enough to stagger.

"We made it back alive." She sounded surprised.

"Of course, we did." Never admit to doubt.

"Looks like we brought friends."

He looked behind her at the horn, that stupid innocuous appendage, and saw the limb peeking out of mid-air, feeling its way around.

"I think that's our cue to leave."

"Not without Nana's recipe." She darted to grab it. The moment it left the pedestal, it set off an alarm. The whole chamber glowed red.

"That's pretty," she declared as everything took on a crimson hue.

"Glad you like it because that means our exit could be tricky."

"It was my recipe," she said with a frown, clutching it tight. "It fell out of my pocket."

"It was found at a demon site."

"It's still mine. Not my fault you and your fancy wizard friends couldn't crack it." How ironic they couldn't decode her sorcery.

"Watch out." The tentacle reached across the floor, seeking them, and she stomped it.

When she would have raised her hand to use magic, he might have yelled, in a rather unmanly fashion, "Don't do it."

She did it. Tossed something energy-based at the portal. While in the very protected vault.

"We need to get out of here." Because if there was one thing the vault didn't like, it was magic being used. Especially combat magic.

He grabbed her hand and pulled her after him, aiming for the exit marked on the wall. A mundane light was their beacon out.

He drew the symbols to open the door as she exclaimed, "Wow, you should see how many tentacles can fit through that rip. I think it's getting bigger."

The door opened with a pressurized hiss, and he emerged to the pointed tips of two blades.

"Don't aim those at me, you idiots," Alistair exclaimed. "One of the artifacts opened a gate. Don't let the monster out."

"Gates cannot be opened inside the vault," proclaimed idiot number one.

"Search them for an artifact." Guard number two tucked his spear into a holder at his back and approached.

Alistair could feel the approaching appendages. Wind, full of heated sand and darkest despair, pushed past him.

"You morons," he declared. "Look behind me."

Before he could move, something shoved, and Alistair tumbled out of the doorway, the unnatural breeze whipping past, followed by a tentacle.

"What is that?" yelled a guard.

"Doesn't matter. Don't let it escape."

Finally, they recognized the true danger. Alistair pulled Willow with him to safety and let the guards handle it.

Whacking it with magic, they cut off pieces

of the probing arm, enough that they could slam the door shut.

Something banged on it.

"Are you going to do something?" Willow hissed.

"Like what? They locked the door."

"What if it escapes?"

He was less worried about the Ceterum than he was about the doorway to that other world. A place best left forgotten.

He pushed away from Willow and approached the wall and guards. "As senior wizard on the scene, I am recommending we employ the obliteration protocol."

"You can't just destroy the vault," the guard exclaimed.

The door at his back boomed and shook. Plaster fell.

Guard number two wasn't as stupid as his friend. "Do it!"

Alistair held up his hands and invoked the magic threaded into the wall, power that wrapped around the entire vault. Once he tripped the right spell, it would react and obliterate everything inside.

Treasure, monster, and even fragile interdimensional rips.

Enacting it would result in committees and paperwork. Alistair hated paperwork. He did it anyway.

The wall flared a bright red and pulsed.

"It's done," he declared.

"Just so you know, when the wizards

question me, I'm gonna tell them you broke the vault," Willow said.

He laughed. "Gotta admit it was fun."

"If that's your idea of a good time, then we have problems."

"We've been in trouble since the demons began their infiltration," he said, sobering.

"That rip went to the demon world, didn't it?"

"It did."

"How did no one know?"

And by no one, she meant how did the wizards not figure it out? He shrugged. "Best guess, when the worlds were out of alignment, the horn remained inert. It probably reactivated when they began rotating in the same sphere again." No need to mention that a certain touch might have set it off.

"So there could be more objects like that? Things that no one even suspects are magic out there in the world."

"Yes."

"And you think the demons will use them."

"I think they'll use any method they can to come to our world."

"But only so long as we're in alignment. Once we move apart, things will go back to normal, right?"

"They will. I just don't know how long that will take."

He led her away from the blackening wall of the vault and the bent-headed murmurs of the guards. As the heat of the intense obliteration fire burned everything into nothingness, so would the wall darken. Only when it crumbled would anyone be allowed to enter and examine the remains.

A few wizards went jogging past, excitement in their expression as they were called to action. They were in the minority. A glance out a window showed others streaming out of the building. Not exactly a brave bunch.

"Shouldn't we stay to answer questions? Won't it look suspicious, us leaving?" she asked.

"Very. I'll just tell them we had important Mago business to attend to."

"And you think they'll buy that?"

"They're too weak and too ill-informed to know any differently."

"That's a rude thing to say about your fellow wizards."

"I wouldn't compare them to me. We are night and day."

"Understatement."

"I'm glad to see you recognize my uniqueness."

"Arrogance."

"Well-earned arrogance."

Her laughter warmed him. "How can I hate you when you say things like that?"

"Why would you want to hate me?" He stopped and forced her to face him.

Her gaze met his, clear and uncertain. "Because if I hate you, then I can't fall for you."

Willow, falling in love with him?

He didn't know what to say.

Chapter Twenty-four

Nothing like telling a guy you liked him first.

And then having him freeze. I wanted to die. Like, seriously, sink into the ground.

What was I thinking? Then again, I wasn't. I—

He swept me into his arms and growled, "It's too late for us both, I think." Alistair kissed me.

Kissed me good.

His lips slanted over mine, caressing and nibbling and touching.

Instant fire licked at my veins, and my skin chafed within my clothes. I tugged at his shirt.

"We're too public," he muttered against my lips.

"Throw in a bonfire, and we can claim it's a heathen witch ritual." I was too aroused for him to want to stop because someone might see and object.

He laughed against my lips. "How about we find a room with a door instead?"

His idea of a room was a utility closet. No window, no light, just a shelving unit and enough space in front of it to tear at each other's clothes.

There was something about the dark, and

doing things by touch alone, that cranked the hot degree up a notch.

Everything seemed twice as intense. The feeling of his lips crushing mine. The stroke of his hands over my skin. Our naked bodies pressed together. Him leaning me against the shelves. Not a comfortable bed.

My body didn't care.

All I knew was desire.

Need for him.

His thigh nudged mine apart and pressed against me.

"You're wet." He sounded so pleased.

"Do something about it," was my smart-ass reply.

"It would be my pleasure."

He dropped to his knees suddenly, and I gasped as I realized his intent.

I had to grab him by the hair to hold myself steady as he nudged his way between my thighs and blew hotly on my sex.

His hands stroked over my thighs, and while I couldn't see them in the dark, I felt the callused skin of his fingers as they dragged over my flesh.

His tongue found and licked me, probing my sex and teasing me. I moaned, and he whispered "Shhh," against my damp lips.

A second moan escaped. As if I could keep quiet.

He lapped me once more, and again. I had one hand fisted in his hair, the other gripping the shelving unit as I rode his tongue, the licking driving me mad.

When I thought I might scream with frustration, he stood. He grabbed me by a leg and hooked it around his hips.

It wasn't high enough. He lifted me and pressed my back against the shelving unit.

The swollen tip of him poked at my lips. I tightened my leg around him, drawing him near, pulling him deep, sighing with the pleasure of having him inside me.

He nudged a little deeper, and I gasped. I loved that he didn't move for a second, just stayed pressed deep inside, letting me enjoy the feel of him.

My arms looped loosely around his neck, I found his lips for a kiss, tasted myself on his tongue as he began to move. His cock rocked into me, deeply each time, sending jolts of pleasure, oh my God, the pleasure.

Then he stopped and set me down on trembling legs, and I mewled, "No."

He wasn't done.

Once again, he dropped to his knees, a supplicant before my altar. His tongue found me. His hands held my thighs wide as he licked me. He flicked my clit with his tongue before sucking it, driving me wild. I could only lean weakly and enjoy it. Then protest as he brought me to the brink and then stopped.

Over and over he did that until I growled, "Don't make me beg."

"I will never make you beg for pleasure," was his promise as he rose and once again slid into me.

The fullness of his throbbing cock was what I craved. He thrust into me, hard, over and over again until I came, my scream caught by his fierce kiss.

And still, I orgasmed, my pussy trembling around his cock as he drove himself in and out, over and over, each thrust hitting my sweet spot, a never-ending bliss.

When he came, it was almost a relief to finally have that boneless pleasure stop.

He collapsed against me, his heavy weight driving me into the shelves, but I didn't mind it. I clutched him tightly, enjoying this rare moment of intimacy with a man.

Until I realized something.

He'd done it again.

Came inside me.

But for some reason, I wasn't as pissed this time. Perhaps it was because I realized this thing between us was stronger than us both. Maybe even meant to be.

Did a sorceress believe in fate?

I know what I didn't believe in, though, and that was a man, even a sexy one with his dick still buried inside me, telling me what to do.

Chapter Twenty-five

"What did you say?" Her words emerged very low and calm, but Alistair knew better.

She's mad.

He heard the controlled rage underneath, yet he still couldn't stop himself. "I am telling you to skip the ball tomorrow tonight."

"Why would you ask me to do that?" she asked. "I have to attend. Coven priestess here. Not to mention, I already replied to my RSVP."

"I don't want you going, though. It's too dangerous."

She snorted. "Do you really think that's a deterrent?"

He slid out of her, not wanting to lose the connection, but, hearing her annoyance, thought it best. "There's word that something might happen at the ball. Something bad."

"If that's the case, why not cancel the ball?"

"Because that would be admitting there are things happening that the TDCM can't control. That no one can control. The various groups are engaged in a game of pretend. None of them want to admit we are in special times. Things need to change."

"Funny you should say that. I was thinking

of change, too. Such as not letting fear control me anymore. I'm going to the ball."

"I forbid it."

As expected, she laughed at him. He felt more than saw her in the dark lunge for the door and open it. Bright hall light lit the inside where his pants were partially down.

She, however, was perfectly dressed and leaving him to the mocking gaze of the wizards just outside.

"Look away." He shot a spell at them as he hurriedly dressed and followed Willow.

Except he never caught up. He was waylaid by idiots wanting to know what had happened in the vault.

Was something taken?

Did they need to arrest the witch?

At that, he barked, "No one is to touch her, or they'll answer to me."

And by answer, he meant kill.

Willow was his.

Best she recognize that. When he finally extricated himself by turning the vault events into a blaming of the TDCM office for not properly checking and securing an activated artifact, thus causing a widespread emergency, he went looking for Willow.

She hadn't gone to her office.

Her assistant Kal hadn't seen her.

Nor had she gone home.

A ping of her location—via a spell cast upon the stray hair he found clinging to his shirt—placed her at her parents' house. Surrounded by all her brothers, it appeared, when he counted cars. Maybe even other relatives.

Perfectly safe.

Yet he didn't want to leave. It felt wrong being away from her. He…missed her.

The realization caused him to curse. How could he miss a woman who constantly vexed him? Who panted so sweetly at his touch?

His phone buzzed. He ignored it. It vibrated again. He took a moment to glance through the messages.

The damned TDCM needed him, but what if she did, too?

His phone rang angrily, and he sighed.

He wouldn't get what he wanted tonight.

Stay safe, Willow. I'll see you soon.

Chapter Twenty-six

Wishful thinking had me peeking out a window, thinking I sensed Alistair nearby.

Stupid. I mean, how would I know if Alistair were stalking me? He'd better not be. I was mad at him. Giving me orders as if he had a right to tell me what to do.

I stroked Whiskers, my little furball left at my parents' house for safekeeping lest a demon try and steal him again. He purred happily in my arms.

I, on the other hand, wasn't as content.

Don't go to the ball indeed. I had to go. Something was afoot. Something more than just the demons.

Secrets. I smelled secrets.

Starting with Alistair. Was he a good guy or a bad guy? What if, by not turning him in, and trusting him—also known as lusting after him— unwittingly brought about the demise of humanity?

Please don't let me be that blurb in the annals of history that said, *Stupid girl, let her hormones get in the way of common sense. Because she didn't stop him, his evil plan succeeded.*

Yet, I didn't get a sense of evil from Alistair. That wasn't to say he was chivalrous hero material. Far from it. He possessed a ruthless core, and I wouldn't want to be the idiot who got in his way or said no.

Which was why I found myself surprised— and fairly disappointed—when he didn't come after me at my parents' place. Sure, it was a wee bit difficult to get in—Mom had a thing for magical booby traps, and Dad loved his gadgets—but what was a little security? He was a Grande Mago, after all.

Alas, I slept undisturbed. The alarms remained untripped. It seemed he wasn't crazy enough to take on my entire family for the sake of one woman.

Alistair also didn't contact me at all the following day.

Not once. He didn't even attempt to reiterate his ridiculous order to stay home from the ball.

Not even to say, "Hey, Willow, how are you doing?"

Not. One. Word.

Asshole.

Who cared about Alistair Fitzroy anyhow? I was Willow Johnson, High Priestess for the Glas Cailleach Coven. I didn't need a man, or wizard, telling me what to do.

So I dressed for the ball. I wasn't about to miss it.

The food is too good to pass up. Apart from excellent noshing, a part of me had a feeling something would happen. Something big. Why else would he warn me away?

I didn't care if he thought it would keep me

safe. For all I knew, he wanted all the glory for himself. Or perhaps he was swinging for the wrong team and worried I'd stop him in his tracks.

Whatever the reason, I would be present and a part of what happened tonight.

I didn't have a super broom to bring me or even a converted pumpkin. My car was recovering—apparently, not happy about the abuse I'd recently put it through—at Dad's old garage where I got a very big glare from my father and a grumbled, "What have you done now?"

I'd gone and done a wizard and now was going to poke him by showing up at the ball. My version of a raised middle finger. Tell me what to do indeed.

Ha. I'd show him.

Ever notice that when you need to dress for a bit of in-your-face revenge, you always looked amazing? I came across as all kinds of awesome in my curve-hugging, eye-popping, purple gown.

I'd even worn sexy underpants. The diamond barrette—courtesy of my dollar store—pinned only the hair at the top of my head. The rest fell over my shoulders and slithered like fiery silk when I moved.

My jeweled wand—my going-out wand as I had laughingly nicknamed it—was tucked in the waist-enhancing sash at my side. For the moment, I was keeping up appearances.

When I strutted in, the high slit in the dress showed off some leg and my startling high heels. I would admit to using a big of magic to keep my balance. One twisted ankle as a teen was enough to prove gravity would always win.

Unlike other guests who arrived—the flying horses pulling a chariot, the aquadome that rolled out of the stretch Hummer and took the mer couple inside—I didn't get a trumpeting announcement.

The doorman—a hulking eight-foot orc who'd actually bathed—took one look at me and snorted. "No humans allowed."

"High Priestess for the Glas Cailleach Coven."

"Human." Even the monsters had disdain for my kind. But I didn't let that bother me, not when I drew gazes the moment I walked into the room.

It might have been the dress. It was anything but subtle. However, it was more likely because I'd chosen to have magic wash around me in a warm, floral-scented breeze, lifting my hair, making anyone who took a deep breath close by suddenly think I was the most awesome thing since they'd learned to deep fry ice cream.

The lusting spell wouldn't last long, but I enjoyed casting it because... *look, everybody.*

No hands.

Indeed, my wand stayed tucked. I didn't move my hands or lips at all, yet no one could deny a cloud of magic followed me.

I could see the puzzled glances as the wizards tried to figure out the trick. Other species were more subtle. I could see their unfocussed gazes as they peered with their othersight. Checking out my aura, which I usually kept tightly wound. Not tonight. Tonight, it shone the same color as my dress. A color none of them had seen before.

A part of me smirked and was tempted to throw out my arms and say, *I'm a sorceress. Welcome to my coming-out ball.*

However, I doubted I'd get a chance to say a word given the thundercloud that moved my way.

Alistair, dressed to the nines in a tuxedo and wearing a mighty scowl, descended on me.

"You," he said when he got close enough.

"Yes, it's me." I batted my thick lashes, spiderweb-woven extensions for the special occasion.

"What happened to staying home?"

"You're not the boss of me," I retorted. Not real mature, but all the other arguments I'd prepared fled when I faced him. *He smells damned good, too.*

"I prefer to think of it more as cooperating since we are partners."

"Partners check in on each other."

"Did you miss me?" he asked.

I tossed my hair. "Not one bit."

"Liar."

"Priceless coming from you. *Fitzroy.*" I emphasized his false name.

His lips twitched. "I see you went with subtlety tonight." His gaze roved my frame, and it took an effort not to cock my hip a little more and thrust out my chest.

"Screw subtlety. You're just mad that the

lowly witch did not listen to the big, bad wizard," I taunted.

"I'm angry because you look fucking fantastic and every male in here has noticed you."

As I expected a chiding or tongue-lashing, the words had me blinking and replying with a very scathing, "What?"

"You are an absolute goddess in that gown. Do you have any idea how many males in this room want you?"

"Uh, none." Seriously, I doubted any of the snobs present were lusting after a human witch.

Alistair thought differently. "They need to realize you're not available."

"But I am. Single, that is."

"No, you're not," he growled. "You're mine."

The possessive words wrapped me in heat. My knees trembled. I know my girly parts swooned into a puddle.

Shocked by his claim, I wasn't prepared for him to grab me in his arms and kiss me.

In public.

Things got kind of quiet around us. Even the music slowed.

I kissed him back and ignored the whispers. When a man kissed you in front of an audience, it meant something.

At least, to me it did.

When he finally let me up for air, he smiled, his gaze smoldering with lust, my panties probably ash from the heat.

"I'm confused. First, you're peeved to see

me. Then, you're happy." Because that wasn't a revolver in his pocket. "I don't get it."

A devilish light danced in his eyes. "I knew you'd come to the ball if I said you couldn't."

"But I was already planning to come."

"Would you have come with me if I'd asked to be your date?"

Yes. No. Maybe. "The politics…"

"Don't mean squat to me." Alistair shrugged. "My way, you arrived full of confidence and fire. Tonight you're not just Willow the coven witch. You're Willow, a woman who doesn't take shit from anyone."

A woman who let her annoyance show an entire room she could do magic. My mouth rounded. "You played me."

He leaned close and brushed the words across my lips. "No, I encouraged you to be who you are."

"I hate you."

"No, you don't. But you can be mad if you'd like. You're hot when you're angry."

"You'll be hot once I set fire to your pants." Said without as much vehemence as he deserved. Hello, the guy had just paid me a compliment.

"You always set fire to my pants," he replied with a chuckle.

"You're a wicked man, Alistair Fitzroy."

"I know." He took a step back and held out his hand. "Shall we dance?"

There was only one reply to that.

I slid my hand into his, and he swept me away.

We danced. And danced.

Alistair whirled me around and around. Swooping. Dipping. Quick stepping. I laughed, and he allowed himself a fierce smile—and a possessive scowl when a few male guests came too close.

A wizard with jealousy issues. I didn't think my panties could get any wetter.

Involved in a fairytale-ish evening, I forgot all about the demons, and my responsibilities. I didn't gab with any of the heads of other groups— although I did offer a few smiles and head bobs. To my surprise, many of them returned it. But I didn't stop to schmooze with anyone at all.

All my attention was focused on Alistair. The wizard/prince making this girl's fantasies come true.

Reading and seeing perfect romantic moments in books and movies didn't prepare you for the breathtaking, giddy happiness of it. Being the focus of a man that you're falling for, flirted with, and catered to was a heady sensation.

I bloomed under his admiration, relaxed, and didn't hold back. I laughed. Smiled. Teased him right back. My body flushed every time he drew me close. My heart pattered faster whenever he dropped a kiss on my lips.

He didn't hide his interest in me.

Everyone noticed. Let them stare at the wizard and the witch cutting up the dance floor, two people on a date where the rest of the world took a backseat.

When I finally begged for a break, because I had a gerbil-sized bladder screaming to go, I walked on a cloud. I was having my princess moment and couldn't wait to get back to Alistair.

It took only moments to relieve myself and wash my hands. I hummed happily as I saw myself in the mirror, eyes bright, smile wide.

I looked so happy.

Like a woman in love.

Er, what?

No point in denying it. I loved Alistair.

And I was beginning to think he loved me.

Stunned by my revelation, I walked out of the bathroom oblivious to everything—which was probably why I didn't see whatever hit me on the back of the head.

Chapter Twenty-seven

Scanning the crowd, Alistair paid only scant attention to the milling guests, the panoply of colors and noise too much for a man who preferred the quiet—and no people.

If Alistair could have his way, he'd be anywhere else, with Willow.

But something was going to happen tonight. He could feel it. Tension thrummed in the air. Other people felt it, too; you could tell by the way they kept glancing around and engaging in hushed whispers.

Then there was Morfeus, who'd winked at him upon his arrival. An expression Alistair didn't trust now that he knew about the corruption of someone highly placed in the TDCM. He didn't worry about possession. Those with magic were immune to that particular curse; however, that didn't mean a wizard couldn't be swayed.

The fact that they'd gotten to Morfeus, and probably others, led Alistair to believe the demons weren't worried about hiding as much anymore. Things were coming to a head.

Speaking of head, he didn't spot a redheaded one returning from the ladies' room. Willow had left some time ago, and while he understood women needed more time to freshen up, this seemed inordinately long.

Too long, and it nagged at him. Seeking her out, though, seemed a little too desperate. Clingy.

A male should never be clingy.

A man should also never ignore the tingling of his gut that said something wasn't right. Alistair began edging his way to the outer rim of the room, past heavily perfumed trolls—who could never completely hide their musky scent. The smell always gave them away even if they remained hidden behind the glamours that made their eight-foot, hulking bodies appear small and svelte. Some species didn't trust the new world and preferred to continue hiding.

Alistair skirted around a group of fairies, already drunk on nectar and shaking their wings hard enough to send glitter flying. Damned stuff never came out.

He barely spared a glance at the glass wall of the giant aquarium; the bright coral inside specially shaped to act as furniture for the aquatic guests.

Alistair had made it to the very edge of the room when he felt it. A shift in the air, a drop in the volume of humming conversations. If an omen had a feeling, this was it.

He turned his head to see the receptionist from the TDCM making his way through the crowd and without having to shove. The wizard moved unimpeded as people stepped out of his way, as if he had a bubble around him pushing them.

I don't see any magic.

Perhaps it was the object he carried. A very charred yet recognizable horn.

This wouldn't be good.

The guy climbed up the steps to the dais where the band played. Without saying a word, they tapered off, and the crowd quieted. In the hush, Alistair could hear the anticipation.

The horn sat flat in the fellow's hands, a burnt husk that crackled with magic. Power Alistair could finally see but only because it was broken.

Not broken enough.

As the guy blew into it, Alistair could see a bubble emerge, a distorted ripple suspended in mid-air. A portal to another world, about four feet wide and eight feet tall. Big enough to cause trouble.

A hand slipped out of the crackling ether first. A human-looking hand. Followed by a humanish body. The fellow, his hair a fiery orange with hints of silver at the temples, wearing an ensemble more suited for the 1700s, landed on the dais and perused the crowd.

"How kind of you to gather in one spot. This will make things easier," said the stranger, rubbing his hands.

"Who are you?" a rather distinguished elf asked, his silver head taller than most, his tone firm yet melodically sweet.

"I am Braxius, from the branch of the Terrible Ones. The descendant of the one you banished, the one called Lucifer." He smiled, his filed teeth deadly as a shark's, his eyes red pits of madness. "I am the last true ruler of the world your kind calls Hell, and now, with my legion behind me, I shall move from that dead land into yours. Bow before your king."

It might have been more impressive if a) people understood exactly who Braxius was—a psychotic inbred despot of a dying land desperate to keep from dying out—and b) if those people weren't rulers in their own right.

As it was, it started with one titter, then a handful, until the whole room erupted in laughter.

Yeah, that really wouldn't go over well.

"Cease at once!" Braxius yelled. When that didn't work, he stood taller, then straighter still, and a black miasma surrounded him, a wispy cloud of magical motes drawn through the rift. Hell might not have trees—anymore—but it had plenty of magic.

"Let us see if you still laugh when you meet my army! It is time to come forth, legion." His voice rang, loud and ominous. "Come feast upon the bodies so kindly being offered."

A black cloud swirled around Braxius, echoing his words before shooting off to cling to the rift, a tear everyone could now see outlined in the air.

A portal that widened.

Really not good.

Yet Alistair didn't move to stop it. It could just be a diversion.

Willow still hadn't reappeared, and given he didn't spot Morfeus…he had a bad feeling. Alistair pushed his way through the riveted crowd—who still didn't grasp the danger—and headed for the hall she'd disappeared down.

When the crowd ooohed, he briefly looked over his shoulder to see why.

The first demon crawled through the rift, a smallish version, sporting stubby wings, horns on its forehead, and a tail. It peered at the crowd and hissed.

The crowd hissed back.

The wizard on stage stumbled to the side when the gaze of the demon turned on him. He held up his hands. "I'm on your side."

The last treacherous words he ever said.

The room went quiet, and all heard the wet slurp as the demon fed, and grew.

Another creature stepped out of the rift. In its claws, another horn, a black one with a wide, fluted end. A warhorn.

The demon held it to his mouth and blew.

A clarion note emerged, strong and never-ending. It echoed through the room, staggering people as it swept through and past them. The sound went on and on, rolling over the surrounding buildings, thundering through neighborhoods. It rolled for miles, Alistair would wager, giving the signal.

The sign for the legion to come forth.

Out they marched from the rip in the air, one by one, demons as depicted in the books, monsters no one had ever imagined, and, worst of all, those who looked just like the humans and elves but with only one thought in mind.

Destruction.

There was no more laughing now. Few screams, too. The species gathered in the room weren't prone to hysteria. They wouldn't have survived long against the humans if they were. Nor did they come to the ball unarmed.

Centuries ago, they'd learned their lesson. Even among allies, sometimes you had to defend.

Blades were drawn, sometimes from the very air itself, and the room swirled with magic.

Blood would be shed this evening, and with so many ready to do battle, Alistair didn't feel compelled to remain. His gut still insisted that this was but a diversionary tactic.

He slipped out of the ballroom as the chaos of battle began and waded through those striving to re-enter to join their friends and allies. While some would flee the violence, many, hamstrung by today's rules, would welcome a chance to unleash their more violent sides. Even the elves, who touted themselves as more evolved, enjoyed a good skirmish.

The path suddenly cleared, and he could see the doors to the facilities. Alistair poked his head inside.

An amethyst-eyed fairy wearing a gossamer-thin gown blinked at him. "You have the wrong facilities, sir."

He ignored her and called out, "Willow, are you in here?"

No reply. Dammit. Where had she gone?

About to leave, a dulcet soft voice said, "Are you looking for the redheaded witch?"

He whirled. "Yes. Have you seen her?"

Wispy hair in baby blue curls bounced as she nodded. "I was on my way in here when I saw her. A gray-haired wizard with the department knocked her out with a good whack to the head in the hall. Said she snuck in."

Morfeus! He fought to keep chill foreboding at bay as he growled. "Which way did they go?"

Thin shoulders lifted and fell. "No idea. They went up the hall, and I came in here. I should rejoin the party."

The damned conscience he'd acquired nudged him. "The ballroom is under attack. By demons."

A human would have screamed and run away. But a fairy was made of sterner stuff, despite what the legends said.

The amethyst gaze turned hard, and she pulled a needle-thin sword from a hidden spot down her spine, between her wings. "About time they finally provided some entertainment for this thing." Off she flitted past him, and he could only shake his head.

Would no one take this seriously?

At least now he knew who had Willow. It didn't reassure, especially given how much Morfeus appeared to hate her. Alistair would have to move fast to save her.

Where would Morfeus have taken Willow? And why?

You know why. Willow was a witch, and guess who needed to feed on them?

The demons needed that magical blood,

and she had more power than most. More than many witches combined. Someone, Braxius or one of his minions, would delight in using her to fuel their existence on this plane.

Since Morfeus couldn't be possessed, that meant he planned to offer Willow to someone else. Someone worth the trouble of performing a kidnapping at a very public event.

"Where did you go?" he muttered out loud. The spell he'd used previously had faded, which meant tracking her down visually since there were too many scents around. Hard stone floors also didn't leave a mark.

The hall extended to the back of the convention center, the bathrooms only a short distance from the kitchens. He went through the swinging door to find it empty. The pots left bubbling on the stove, food, partially chopped on the counters. Massive trays loaded with snacks.

They looked and smelled delicious. He was tempted to snare a handful on his way out the door, but juggling food while fighting? A male should have standards.

Alistair emerged into a fragrant herb garden, vacant of anyone, the air redolent with the smell of the plants.

The power of it masked every scent. His head turned side to side. Which way had they gone? Had Morfeus left the house or—

Lightning crackled overhead. Quick, short stabs of light, one after another. Peeking upwards, he saw nothing on the heavily sloped rooftop.

The jagged streaks kept coming, but less

overhead and more to his left. Alistair took off at a steady pace, vaulting over the small gate that bordered the garden. He landed on a cultivated lawn that went down in tiers, almost like giant, green steps. The far edges of it were bordered by trees through which peeked fairy lights—which couldn't start fires—and the faint hum of music. Some guests had chosen to party outside. The dryads had gotten shy since their wide-scale murder by the forest industry.

Having arrived when it was still light, he knew a small lake, little more than a pond really, sat at the bottom of the tiers. The water shimmered during the day, a clear and clean blue with a sandy bottom. Night had fallen, which meant the only light came from glowing glass globes that did little to pierce the foggy morass forming over the lake.

Where he'd grown up, thick fog, the kind that you couldn't see your hand in, didn't bode well. Not at all.

But the worst thing about those kinds of thick mists? Sound. Sound always seemed amplified. The screams echoing louder and longer. The chill in your bones not from the cold.

This fog didn't have screaming—yet. However, Alistair did hear voices, stilted pieces of conversation.

"…time you…cleanse the…filthy hearth witch."

Found you.

Alistair made straight for the fog.

A warm wind hit him, redolent with the scent of brimstone and ash. Another rift had formed.

The worlds had aligned even more, the holes between them growing in number. He could only hope this was the apex of the alignment. According to research—unverified and rare—once the peak was reached, the worlds would quickly fall out of sync, which stymied the more scientifically inclined because of how long it took to reach this point.

Decades of moving into position, the thin spots were barely noticed unless by accident. But with the planes perfectly aligned, even the blindest demons could spot a chance to cross over, and given humanity's dense population, they'd find a body to possess for survival.

It had to be stopped.

If the people of this world can stand against the legion tonight, then maybe there is a chance for tomorrow.

Clenching his fists at his sides, Alistair began to draw power to himself, sucking it from the very air, drawing it from the unnatural mist even, clearing it the more he siphoned the magic creating it.

As the fog receded, so appeared those he sought.

First thing he noted, a mauve heap on the ground. Willow, not moving at all. The cause? A smirking Morfeus, who stood over her, hands raised.

You'll die for that.

Of more concern, the whirlpool in the center of the lake, a yawing hole from which rumbled forth a noise that chilled his blood.

Something was coming. The whirlpool was a rip.

It swirled, churning faster and faster, growing in size, yet nothing appeared. Nothing flew out. Perhaps the water stopped it.

Then what of that sound, a low, ululating cry, a tremble in the air?

What would emerge?

He expected tentacles, something to come waggling out of there, an ancestor of the Kraken that had crawled onto land. Perhaps from that hole would appear another of those red-haired bastards because Braxius certainly wasn't the only one. The children and grandchildren of the original Lucifer had multiplied over the centuries. Lucifer had been prolific in ensuring the continuation of his bloodline after they banished him. Just like not all his children were born from his kind.

Fornication and magic brought forth all kinds of heirs. All dangerous. All powerful.

In the case of the giant line Lucifer had seeded those many, many years ago, they were huge.

Big fingers, larger than Alistair's thigh, gripped the edge of the water. Yes, gripped. Magic could do so many, many things, especially when you had lots of it to play with.

Size did matter.

Speaking of sizeable, a huge beast began to heave itself out of the whirlpool, the arms bulging as it strained to pull itself up, the tips of curved, ebony horns protruding.

An old one from the time of the goliaths

had stirred. They were supposed to remain asleep.

"What have you done?" Alistair snapped at Morfeus.

Turning to face him, Morfeus smiled, and Alistair could see the madness of fanaticism peeking out of his eyes. "He's coming. The Dark Lord who will cleanse this Earth."

"That's not the Dark Lord, you idiot." Just a massive beast, Hell's version of a dinosaur, with a modicum of intelligence.

"The Dark Lord will need soldiers in this world."

"Soldiers are wasted. The Dark Lord can't survive on this plane," Alistair stated. Those who lived in the other dimension couldn't just walk into this world, not without suffering—unless they took over a body or ate the right kind of magic.

His gaze strayed to Willow with her brilliant red hair. A human with epic magic. Possibly descended from Lucifer himself before he'd been banished. A perfect blood match to those seeking to cross over.

Shit.

Alistair moved forward, raising his hands, two glowing fists of mauve magic, only to have Morfeus cackle. "No need for you to feed the Dark Lord's pet. Her blood will do."

"You idiot. You don't understand what you're unleashing."

"And you're obviously not who I thought you were." Morfeus's gaze narrowed. "You have an unnatural bond with the witch. She's obviously cast a spell on you."

"No spell, asshole," snapped Willow, pushing herself up on her elbows. "It's called being a decent human being."

"Human?" Morfeus laughed. "He's not human. Hasn't been since he crossed over a few years back. Alistair here is a demon. A highly placed one, too. Here to pave the way for our coming."

A shocked green gaze met his. "Is that true?"

He wanted to deny it, to lie. To do anything but see the betrayal in her gaze.

Except the beast chose that moment to heave his head and shoulders from the whirlpool and open his mouth to roar.

Chapter Twenty-eight

Freaking on your boyfriend because he never admitted his demon heritage was important; however, even more important was the giant monster leering at me, his thick lips stretched wide, his teeth, two layers of them, jagged and I'd bet sharp.

Add in Morfeus clapping his hands and saying, "I brought the witch for you to dine on," didn't help.

Excuse me. I wasn't anybody's snack. I jumped to my feet, meaning to back away from the lake's edge, in the opposite direction of the swirling whirlpool birthing the demon.

Morfeus darted behind me. A shove propelled me forward, and I whirled to glare at the bane of my existence.

"You are starting to piss me off," I snapped.

Morfeus spat, "You have been a thorn in my side for weeks now, hearth witch. I look forward your death."

"I'm not a witch, dammit." At a time like this, I wished I'd invested in some kind of super sorceress outfit. I mean, that evil chick in *Suicide Squad* had it going on with her impressive smoky loincloth dress. All I had was a rather ragged-looking gown that no amount of dry cleaning would fix, and hair that had lost most of its lift and hung drunkenly over my left ear.

The leer on Morfeus's lips met my fist.

I'm pretty sure I split it, given the blood smearing his mouth. "You filthy witch."

"Again. I'm not a witch. I'm a sorceress. Which, in case you're not informed, is better than a wizard."

Morfeus laughed. "As if someone lowborn and common could aspire to that kind of—"

While I usually loved a good villain speech, I'd had quite enough of this pompous asshat. I grabbed Morfeus in a magical fist and lifted him.

He stopped what he was saying, and his eyes widened. "Put me down!"

"Me?" I batted my lashes, trying to ignore the fact that one still had the false webs and the other one didn't. "How can it be me? You said I had no real magic." I waggled him up and down, and he screamed—which was quite satisfying.

Lightning continued to crackle, and I tried to keep an eye on the water, the swirling hole having enlarged, almost reaching the lake's edge. At least the monster seemed unable to yank his giant body out, but he was trying, pulling himself hand over hand, gripping the liquid as if it were solid.

"Release me!" yodeled Morfeus, his pale complexion quite red.

"Are you sure?" I smiled. "If you say so." I tossed him. Let him completely go and watched as he sailed in an arc and hit the water.

The current immediately caught him and drew him toward the eye of the vortex.

Morfeus wouldn't be calling me a witch anymore. I might have felt bad but…nah. The guy got what he deserved.

I turned to face Alistair. "You!" I jabbed a finger at him. "You lied to me. You said you weren't a demon."

"I'm not. Mostly. I don't turn into anything, if that's what you're asking. My blood is purer than most."

"What does that mean?"

"I don't have time to explain right now."

"Try," I snapped.

"My family is one of the originals banished. Given our powers and even our appearance are affected by intermixed couplings, they were very careful to not mix our blood to the point where we lost our roots."

"Why were you banished?"

"My people were bad, and that was their punishment."

"Why are you here? Are you part of this plot to invade and take over bodies?"

He shook his head. "Not anymore."

"What's that supposed to mean?"

"I'm not the person I was when I first got here. I don't want what the legion does."

"What do you want then?" I asked as the wind tugged at my dress.

"Do we really have to discuss this now?" he asked, flicking a glance over my shoulder.

"Don't try to avoid the issue. Don't think I don't see what you were doing. You befriended me so you could get me to the ball and feed me to that!" I jabbed a finger behind me.

"No, I befriended you because you were connected to the case. I fell for you after that."

Alistair had fallen for me? "So you don't want the demon to eat me?" A hopeful flutter thumped inside my chest.

"Of course I don't. You're mine, Willow."

Good grief, those were some sexy words. I batted my one thick lash and must have failed miserably at flirting because Alistair didn't even smile.

"The colossus is almost out of the hole. Get behind me," Alistair commanded.

Cute. "I don't need you to protect me."

"Protect you?" He snorted. "Perish the thought. I don't like the way he's ogling you." Alistair scowled.

Sure enough, the monster leered at me. Not sexually, I might add, more in an I-want-to-crunch-her-into-little-bits stare.

"Don't you even think about it," I snapped. "I'm busy having a conversation with my boyfriend."

Alistair snorted. "You do realize he doesn't care."

Obviously not, because the oversized demon hissed at me.

"Don't you sass me." I pulled at the power pulsing in the air all around and lobbed magic at it. A great big ball of sizzling power. The damned thing opened his mouth and swallowed it. Kind of demoralizing.

The giant demon—possibly the granddaddy of demons—was halfway out of the swirling morass and bulging in places that shouldn't bulge. He seemed bigger now. His reach had definitely gotten longer.

I lobbed another ball of magic at him. The demon caught it mid-air and popped it into his mouth.

Alistair yelled, "Stop feeding him."

Um, good plan given the demon had just bumped up a size. His arms, especially, got longer, the fingers swishing overhead.

I should take Alistair's advice and get out of there.

Run from the huge menace to this world. The coven didn't have many codes. Heck, I didn't have a ton either, but there was one thing I did believe in.

Doing the right thing.

That involved dealing with this monster before he could fully come into our world. The good news? My magic bulk-up of his body had wedged him in the hole.

The bad news?

Giant freaking demon.

"How do we kill it?" I asked, running left to avoid the slap of a hand on the shore. Water sprayed.

"Cut off its head."

I peeked at the giant head, which required us crossing water, and… I shook a negative. "That ain't happening. What's plan B?"

Alistair opened his mouth to reply. I never heard the answer seeing as how I kind of had a problem.

Dodging hands was all well and good, except for the fact that Granddaddy Demon also had a tail. I didn't expect one to come snaking out of nowhere to curl around me, a tight vise that squeezed the air from my lungs.

The damned thing was strong. It lifted me off the ground, and no amount of kicking could dislodge me from its grip. Despite the futility of it before, I tried magic again. This time, the demon didn't bother eating it. He let it hit him in the shoulder, where it fizzled on its skin before being absorbed.

He grew.

The big monster cackled, his low rumbled, "More," very chilling.

Alistair was losing his shit, which was kind of hot. He had out his big sword—the glowing kind, not the one between his legs—and he waved it around, slicing into the monster's flesh, and I might have been more optimistic about my chances if those wounds didn't immediately heal over.

Alistair didn't let that small setback stop him. He swung over and over again. I'd never seen a man more intent on saving me.

Hopefully, it would count as points in his favor when my family found out that Alistair was descended from demons because…guess who was charging down the lawn?

I couldn't help but mutter, "Stupid, meddling family." But, sometimes, intrusive could be good.

Mom, wearing the robe she usually kept hidden—one woven of silver unicorn hair that I suddenly coveted because she looked damned impressive—led the charge with an orange kitten clinging to her shoulder.

My dad trotted at Mom's heels, holding, of all things, a mega-sized wrench—spelled to act kind of like Thor's hammer.

Then you had my six brothers, their faces more serious than usual, ready to kick the ass of the demon bugging their little sister.

Damn, I loved my crazy family.

A few yards before the water's edge, they linked hands, a coven of seven, with my dad standing guard, ready to whack anyone, or anything, that tried to disturb them.

I felt compelled to yell, "That thing eats magic to get bigger."

"Not all magic," my mom countered. She closed her eyes and pulled. I could almost see the esoteric forces in the area siphoning in her direction, pulling it away, even from the monster, enough that he shrank a bit.

The demon noticed and let out a yell as he slipped a bit into the hole.

The pulling continued, my mother's voice the drawing spindle that wound magic around it like a fine thread.

Despite the dancing spots in front of my eyes, I watched what my mom was doing. Could see the tendrils of magic spinning out from her spool and weaving into something new as she began to sing, each note dragging and shaping the power in the air, multitasking, pulling magic and shaping it.

But the demon wasn't about to give in easily. He lifted a hand and something dark shot forth, tangling the skeins of magic. The spool stopped spinning as Mom fought to regain control. She tugged. The demon pulled back, an invisible tug of war that saw my mother straining, even with the aid of my brothers.

They needed help, and Alistair noticed. He joined my family, actually placed his hand inside Oak's, and damned if he didn't add his own magical voice to the mix. It added an interesting resonance to the pattern, one that provided a shield to what Mother did. The spool began to spin again, pulling in the threads to weave her other spell.

Yet their combined actions didn't stop the tail from dangling me over the water, pulling me over the eye of the maelstrom where I got a close-up view of a giant maw filled with teeth. *Please let my death be quick*. I didn't want to know what it felt like to be chewed. I closed my eyes because I really didn't want to see myself digested.

Hope seemed futile. A partial coven of eight, while powerful enough for most things, would not be enough to combat this.

What if that eight were multiplied?

More voices suddenly joined the mix, and the air filled with sound. High and fluting notes, low and timbered. My skin prickled with the intensity of the building magic.

I dared to open my eyes to see people moving down the lawn, arms open wide, joining their voices to my mother's.

I knew many of those faces, people I'd met over the years, from elves to fairies, even the troll whose bridge I'd helped rid of crack-smoking transients.

All of them using their own skills to pull all the magic they could muster into the spool, feeding my mother's spell. Helping. Helping *me*.

It made a witch who wasn't a witch feel loved.

It made Granddaddy Demon angry, especially because some of the magic they inhaled came from him. He began to lose more of his size. The beast shuddered and bellowed as smoke rose from his bubbling skin. He heaved and strained to get out of the hole, but the whirlpool kept pulling him down. Which meant I was getting yanked.

I dangled over the whirlpool in the middle of the lake. Could look down and see past the eddying current, past the bobbing head of Morfeus at the bottom end of the cone. I could see into Hell itself.

One visit was enough.

The singing on shore faltered as one voice broke off.

"Willow." Alistair called for me, disrupting the siphon of magic.

As soon as he did, the whole spell wobbled, and the demon found his balance. He began to climb the water again. Freakier, I could still see below him, and another giant figure beginning to rise.

They had to close this hole before we were overrun with giant, hungry demons, but they wouldn't while I dangled over it.

I did the only thing I could do. I yanked the one pin left in my hair free, sending it tumbling, and stabbed the tail with it. Over and over again. The demon bellowed, but the appendage loosened and dropped me, plummeting me into Hell.

Alistair yelled, "No!"

My family screamed, too.

I closed my eyes, waiting to be digested, only...

Something hit me, grabbed me in furry claws, and jerked as it fought to rise with my weight.

Fur with a hint of spice and milk brushed my face, and I wondered what strange creature caught me. A beast not strong enough to pull us out of the vortex.

"Give it magic, Willow," someone yelled. I wondered at the odd instruction yet listened, pushing some magic at the thing holding me. The jerking motion evened, and the sucking lessened. The body with me in its grip stopped moving with a hard jolt. Opening my eyes, I first noted the orange chest, the fur on it thick and soft. Then the size of that chest.

It took a few blinks to take in the fact that my itty-bitty kitty was an interesting mix of gargoyle and cat.

Glowing yellow eyes perused me from a face with flatter features, more teeth, and a tuft of orange hair between the ears. Leathery brown wings projected from the back. The torso was covered in fur, even the long tail.

My kitten was a demon…who'd saved me.

"Someone is getting a great big can of tuna to himself," I said, hugging him. I got a rumbling purr in reply.

Granddaddy Demon roared, and I peeked over Whiskers to see him scrabbling at the whirlpool's edge.

That was when the spell my mother wove slapped him. It slammed down like a shield, a lid covering a simmering pot.

It crushed the demon's fingers, bonked him on the head, and he couldn't hold on. The monster lost his grip and fell. The spell shield kept pushing down, filling in the hole, causing the whirlpool to wobble, the spinning becoming uneven.

The chanting and the magic didn't stop there. It kept building, stronger and stronger overhead, tugging at the forces causing the rift, using the rip's own power against it. I saw crackling light snapping from the hole. Electrical currents and winds buffeting the air around.

Strong arms scooped me from behind. "We need to move away, now."

Alistair took off running, but I knew we'd never make it far enough.

Someone screamed, "Take cover." Since there was nothing in sight, I improvised and spun a shield, one big enough for two people and a, once again tiny, kitten.

The world exploded. At least that was what it felt like. The ground vibrated. My teeth chattered. Whiskers yowled as lake water rained all around us, and Alistair hugged me tightly.

Kept holding me even when the ground stopped trembling and cheering erupted. We'd won the evening.

We'd shut the hole to Hell.

And I was being hugged by a demon.

A demon who'd tried to save me at the cost of himself.

A demon my family was advancing on, hands raised in possible violence.

I pushed out of Alistair's arms and popped to my feet to stand in front of him, hands on my hips. "Don't you even think of touching him."

Oak didn't take his glare off Alistair. "He's one of *them*. I felt it in the circle."

"He's nothing like those other demons," I protested.

"He's not human."

"He doesn't have a tail," I supplied, trying to be helpful.

"No tail, no horns, and yet he's right. I am not human," Alistair supplied. "I am from that place you've been calling Hell, brought over a few years ago by my aunt who was one of the first to discover a rift back when they were rare. We thought her lost until she returned after a few decades."

"This has been happening for decades?"

"The worlds have been aligning slowly, the

holes rare until now. It's why you've seen so few incursions until recently."

"But she managed to go back and find you." I still tried to understand.

"My aunt returned to find allies. She brought me and a few others over to help stem the invasion."

"Brought over!" her brother interrupted. "You're a demon, unable to live in our world, which means you killed someone to stay. Took over their body."

"Actually, this is my form. I managed to complete the ritual required to walk this plane."

"Because you sucked some witches dry," Rowan snapped.

"I did." Alistair did not deny it, nor did he sound apologetic. "Blood, a lot of it, is needed to transform us enough to be able to walk the Earth."

"Like a vampire," I interjected. "And I don't see anyone lining up to kill them all."

"They're not trying to take over the world," Ash argued. "We should kill him and her hell-spawn kitten, too."

Whoa, now they were just getting silly. I crossed my arms. "No one is killing Alistair or my cat. In case you hadn't noticed, they both saved my life."

"They're demons."

"They're mine"—I wagged a finger—"and I love them, so if you want to see them dead, you'll have to go through me." I narrowed my gaze and balled my fingers into fists.

For a moment, my oldest brother held my

gaze, and then he smirked and held out his hand. "Told you she was in love with the wanker. Cough it up."

Only as money exchanged hands did I realize they'd fucked with me. "Does this mean you're not going to kill him?"

"We don't kill allies," Banyan said with a snort. "But we will expect him to spill everything he knows."

Manipulated by my family. I glared at my mother. "Aren't you going to do something about this?"

She clapped her hands. "Indeed, I shall. I'll get started on the wedding menu right away."

"Wedding?" I repeated.

"Daddy will take care of the limo for you, or would you prefer something more old-school like a carriage with horses?" she said, tapping her chin. "I'm owed a few favors. We might be able to get some with wings."

"What wedding?" I yelled. "A second ago, these idiots were talking about killing Alistair."

"You know we were just teasing," Rowan interjected. "Just making sure he has good intentions toward you."

"Which is why he's going to marry you," Sylvan added. "Or else." A fist met a palm with a meaty smack.

"Better wed you soon or there will be an issue with him defiling our little sister." More glares all around aimed at Alistair.

"What they all said." Father tapped his wrench against his thigh for emphasis.

A sigh escaped me. "Stop it. All of you. This is so embarrassing. My love life is none of your business."

"Marry me." The words came from Alistair, and I whirled to see him looking amused.

I scowled. "You're only asking because my brothers want to murder you."

"No, I am asking because I find myself in love with you and determined to make you mine."

I might have thrown myself at him. I certainly gave my brothers, who thought it funny to make gagging noises as I kissed my fiancé, the finger.

My fiancé.

Eek.

I was going to be a bride—which, of course, sent Kal over the moon with dress shopping plans, and my mother made the mother of all Costco runs for supplies.

But that was later. First came the interrogation.

Chapter Twenty-nine

The questioning could have been worse. It helped that so many things had happened that folks were less concerned about what Alistair was and more about the fact that Morfeus and other TDCM employees—aka wizards—were subverted.

But that wasn't to say that everything was rosy. Alistair had been outed as a hybrid form of demon, but not everyone was surprised by his existence. His aunt Jas'a'meen Ba'ak'ra, the first one to truly infiltrate this dimension, had been slowly preparing for their arrival. The female, who'd created a life for herself in this world—and allowed her grandchild to call her Meemaw—was part of the highest council in existence. She was the one who'd brought Alistair and others over, showed him the beauty of this world, then tasked the former soldier—a lowly seventh son of a seventh son—with keeping this world safe.

In the early dawn, his aunt, who'd been present at the ball and instrumental in them pushing back the demonic horde, sent everyone home. There would be time to rehash events and plan for the next invasion—because they hadn't seen the last of the demons.

Nor had they killed all those who came

through. Two vampires had lost their human companions, now suspected of being possessed. The cage of canaries in the kitchen, meant to fill a pie, also gone.

Add in who knew how many had come through in that wave when the horn had put out its call...

The war to save Earth had begun, and Alistair knew there would be no avoiding the questions. Especially from the woman he'd soon marry.

This time, she didn't protest when he insisted they take his truck. Only as they were buckled, her demon cat in her lap, did the torrent of questions begin. "Do you mean to tell me, all this time, you've been looking for a way to stop the demon invasion?" Willow looked confused as Alistair pulled away from Atlantis.

"My aunt is the one who convinced me to do something to save this plane. The wars in my world destroyed what was once a lush land. It wasn't always a hell dimension. Lucifer began the corruption there after his banishment."

"As in *the Lucifer*? He's real?"

"Not in the way the Bible depicts. For one thing, he's not an angel, although he can project wings."

"You keep saying banished. Are you implying that demons and Lucifer originated here?"

"He and his followers committed too many crimes. Rather than perform genocide on a race, they were given the choice of exile. My ancestors moved to a new dimension, one beautiful and lush, then proceeded to repeat the past and destroy it. The demons are what Lucifer and people became. They had to change in order to survive in Hell."

"Why don't you look like a demon?" Willow squinted at him. "Do you shift like a Lycan? Do you have horns and a tail?"

His lips quirked. "Not all of us changed. Those with the strongest magic retained our human aspect."

"If you're so human, then why did you need witch blood?"

"Because, despite retaining our outward appearance, inside, we changed too much. Adapted to our environment, I guess you would say. In order to survive on Earth, we had to re-adapt again. The quickest way was by imbibing the blood of a descendant."

"And by descendant you mean someone with magic."

"Exactly." What he didn't say was that they couldn't just imbibe the blood of any magic user. Those with elven blood only partially satisfied their need. They needed a descendant of Lucifer or his ilk, the so-called witches whose ancestors had borne children from the banished ones, to truly survive.

"Are you descended from Lucifer?"

"Yes. All the major families left are somehow related to him. All striving for his approval."

"You speak as if he's still alive."

"He might be. He disappeared a long time

ago. Some say he went off to die. Others say he's waiting for the right time to return."

"What do you think?"

"I think the world is better off thinking he's dead. He didn't sow a positive legacy."

"You turned out all right."

"By accident. Before coming to your world, I was as violent and bloodthirsty as they came. Everything was about advancing myself in the family. Only once I came into your world and truly understood the possibilities did I change."

"What possibilities?"

"A life that wasn't all about battle and destruction." A life that could involve love.

"So you made it your mission to try and stem the invasion. Why not tell us? Enlist our help?"

"We have been trying, slowly. But as you heard, many take offense to the fact that we need blood, magical blood, to survive."

"Do you need blood forever?"

He shook his head. "No. After a while, our bodies adjust, and your environment is no longer poisonous. However, before we reach that point, we need a lot."

"So you killed people."

"I haven't. It takes longer, but the same result can be achieved with measured amounts from a strong witch. Some, though, don't want to wait. They take too much and kill the donor. Exactly how welcome do you think we'd be if people knew?"

"Complicated."

"It is," he agreed.

"I should probably be more shocked by it, yet I can't fault you for doing what you needed to do to survive. Maybe we've been going about this demon thing all wrong. What if we found a way to help them survive in our world without killing?"

He snorted. "Most of them are past the point of reasoning. Inbreeding and upbringing have made them violent tools."

"Is this your way of saying you're unique?"

"Very. But, then again, so are you." She was a bright and shining prize he'd never expected to find. In his world, affection was seen as weakness. Marriages were made for alliance and strength.

But this was a new world. A new chance. And he was ready to try something new. To love and be loved.

"What do you say we go back to my place and get cleaned up?" she asked.

Meow.

He frowned at the cat who was not a cat.

"Don't worry. I haven't forgotten about some treats for my big hero of the day," she said, baby-talking her pet. She snuggled it close before giving its belly a rub.

A loud purr erupted.

Alistair could have sworn the damned thing smirked at him. It could smirk all it wanted. *I will be the one sinking balls deep into her later.*

He made record time to her place, the fact that she kept petting the kitten in her lap an incentive to have that petting transferred to him.

He wanted to be touched. Never mind that

the world was dealing with a demon outbreak. Who cared if the biggest demon of all might be looking for another portal in? Dawn crested bright with possibility.

He and Willow would deal with the fate of the world later. After he'd made her his.

Entering the house, after she'd taken down her wards, he made a beeline for the kitchen and had the can of tuna opened before she'd even walked into the room with her cat. He held it out.

"Feed it. I'll go start the shower."

It pleased him to notice she didn't waste time following. He'd only managed to strip off his soiled dress shirt when she entered the bathroom and closed the door.

Then stripped, her gaze holding his.

There were all kinds of things he could have said in that moment. None of them could have conveyed strongly enough how he felt.

Love seemed too small a word.

He held out his arms, and she stepped into them, hugging him close. He'd almost lost her today. Almost lost this vibrant, perfect woman.

He kissed her and would have devoured more than her mouth, but she shoved at him. "I reek of demon tail."

He chuckled. "Get in the shower. I'll wash."

And he did, on his knees, a worshipper with soapy hands, cleansing every inch of her body. Marking her with his touch.

She moaned and sighed as he teased her, eyes closed, and her head tilted back. The bench in her shower provided a perfect spot to park her so she wouldn't fall. He knelt between her legs, and she clasped her legs around his waist.

She pulled him close, her moist core pulsing against his lower belly. It put her breasts at just the right height. He latched on to a pert nipple and tugged it.

A noise escaped her, one of pleasure. Her legs wrapped tighter, pressing her sex harder against him.

As he teased the nub with his mouth, he cupped her ass, kneading and playing with the cheeks. She squirmed and moaned at his touch, and it drove him mad with desire.

I want to taste her. With the water of the shower pounding his back, he kissed his way down over her ribs. Her tight vise loosened, allowing him to keep going, kissing her belly before nuzzling her mound.

She spread her legs wide for him, exposing her sex in all its silken glory. He traced the delicate edge of a quivering lip. Felt her shudder.

He pressed his mouth to her and licked, sucked at her sweet honey. Lapped at the proof of her desire for him.

"Alistair." It was his name she moaned as her body quivered. That she screamed as he flicked his tongue again and again over her clit, bringing forth her orgasm.

As she moaned in pleasure, her body shuddering from her first climax, he stabbed his tongue inside her, feeling the quivering waves of her pleasure.

The first of what he hoped would be many

orgasms.

As her body calmed, he worked to bring it to a fever pitch again. He teased her clit. Already swollen, her nub stuck out from its hood, and he tongued it relentlessly. He lapped at her, feeling her pleasure building, coiling, readying itself for a second eruption.

When she skirted too close to the edge, he paused to blow on it, drawing a tortured moan from her lips. A quiver rocked through her body.

Time for something different. He stood and drew her up to her feet, but her legs were weak from pleasure.

"Hold on," he ordered her, lifting her so that his cock aligned with her sex. The tip of him pushed at her, and before he could tease her some more, she wrapped her legs around his waist and sheathed him.

The heat of her pulsed around him, tight and blissful. Control eluded him as his fingers dug into her ass cheeks.

But she wasn't about to let him take control. He might have been the one holding her, but she was the one bouncing on his shaft, her muscles squeezing him, the smooth silk of her flesh rubbing.

He turned enough that he could press her back to the wall, only then did he have the right angle to piston her. His cock thrust deep, hard, hitting her sweet spot over and over.

She trembled in his arms. Her body tensed. With a sharp cry, she came, her channel fisting his cock, drawing forth his own climax. He thrust deep, one final time, marking her with his seed.

Hopefully life.

Giving him the best reason of all to fight his past.

Love.

Epilogue

The demon problem didn't end at that lake or in the ballroom, despite how many holes were closed and demons slew.

Too many rips had opened. Too many of the parasites, those too changed to use their own body, had come through.

The good news? Most died right away, unable to find a proper host or the right kind of blood to sustain them.

The bad? Enough managed to survive that there was a danger in the world. Especially since the planets were still aligned and would be for some time to come. We might have reached a peak, but it was far from over.

And I was one of the ones fighting to save our world.

However, I'd earned a bit of respite, given Alistair and I, along with my brothers, who insisted on helping, had recently cleaned out another haunted house and the demons that inhabited it.

Whiskers purred in my lap as I stroked his fur.

Alistair grimaced. "You're coddling the creature."

"Yup."

"It's a demon."

"Yup." It was. Stuck in a kitten body. My kitten.

"Do you know how jealous the other covens will be when they find out I've got a demon as a familiar?" One that I fed bits of blood to help curb his hunger. But I didn't tell Alistair that. He'd probably forbid it.

"He's a lower-caste demon. Barely cognizant."

"And your point is?" I asked with a pointed stare.

He sighed. "Exactly why do I love you again?"

"Because I'm awesome."

"At driving me insane."

"Sexy."

"And yet you're not naked using that against me."

Alistair teased, but he wouldn't get the last laugh.

"I can't believe you're arguing with a pregnant woman."

It took a moment for it to sink in. And when it did, Alistair Fitzroy—whose real name was Al'stayr Asm'odeus—almost fainted.

He recovered quickly enough that he bellowed, quite loudly, "I'm going to be a father!"

"To twins," I added.

And then he did faint. *Thump.*

I clucked my tongue as I continued to pet my demonic cat. "Big, bad wizard my ass." Good thing I loved him. More than anything in this world. A world that needed more heroes—and demons like Alistair.

The End – unless you really loved it and a great idea smacks me upside the head. Then maybe, just maybe, some of Willow's brothers should get a story...What do you think?

For updates or to get to know me, visit my website, EveLanglais.com

Lightning Source UK Ltd.
Milton Keynes UK
UKHW02f1816090418
320769UK00001B/50/P